# Viagro Blue

# Viagro Blue

By 44288
Ohio Mental Patient

Edited from the original manuscript and
Presented by Perry Aayr

Writers Club Press
San Jose  New York  Lincoln  Shanghai

# Viagro Blue

All Rights Reserved © 2002 by Edward L. Beardshear

No part of this book may be reproduced or transmitted in any form or by any means, graphic, electronic, or mechanical, including photocopying, recording, taping, or by any information storage retrieval system, without the permission in writing from the publisher.

Writers Club Press
an imprint of iUniverse, Inc.

For information address:
iUniverse, Inc.
5220 S. 16th St., Suite 200
Lincoln, NE 68512
www.iuniverse.com

Any resemblance to actual people and events is purely coincidental.
This is a work of fiction.

ISBN: 0-595-24624-9 (pbk)
ISBN: 0-595-74284-X (cloth)

Printed in the United States of America

# Contents

| | |
|---|---|
| Preface | vii |
| Viagro 1 | 1 |
| Viagro 2 | 25 |
| Viagro 3 | 47 |
| Viagro 4 | 67 |
| Viagro 5 | 89 |
| Viagro 6 | 111 |
| Viagro 7 | 133 |
| Viagro 8 | 159 |
| About the Author | 179 |

# Preface

Dear Reader,

Over thirty five years ago when Viagra was absolute and total science fiction, 44288, an Ohio Mental Patient, and author of what I have to believe is one of the best attempts at the Great American Novel (GAN) of the last fifty years, 44288's stunningly original *Some Die Mad*, conceived of this remarkable side splitting story about a little blue pill experimental trial which hoped to produce a male erection that goes terribly wrong and virtually destroys (or creates?) the life of one poor insurance actuary named Millard Fillmore.

The story of who I am (Perry Aayr) and why I get to present this work and edit it from the original manuscript is the subject of three long Prefaces in all the *Some Die Mad* Books, including *Gandy Dancing*, *Auschwitz, Ohio, The Place To Wait* and *Islands In Time*. You can read a full account there.

But long story short, I rescued the entire output of this artistic and literary phenomenon before it was all destroyed. I tracked him down after meeting him once from the first feature story I ever wrote as a journalist in the 1960's. The feature was a piece on art therapy coming to Columbus State Hospital and ran page one in the old Hartley Newspapers flagship edition, The Hilltop Record. I not only met 44288 and saw his paintings, I recalled he told me he was actually a writer and was going to attempt to write the GAN. This was not a crazy for the times despite the locale. Every ink-stained wretch in every pub in every college town in the nation wanted to do the same thing but damn few ever tried. Trust me, I know.

In retirement, I asked myself: Wonder if he wrote it?

So I searched and tracked him down and eventually found this treasure trove of artistic and literary works and rescued it all from the furnace. It was in the nick of time. This gold mine of first class artistic endeavors took up nearly half a basement and included book after book of fiction and non fiction literature, oil paintings, sculptures, plays, poetry, pen drawings, charcoals, experimental pieces in art and literature, even children's books. This treasure trove was stored and hidden by the family out of shame. Most work was submitted for publication by its author rarely. Virtually anything in those years coming in over the transom and hitting the slush pile was ignored and shunned by an industry by then already intent on deflecting authors rather than actually publishing an unknown.

44288 didn't survive his illnesses and the "treatments" of the time. He suffered alcoholism, anxiety neurosis and institutionalization, all of which caused him to be needlessly hospitalized for ten years at Columbus State Hospital and all of which eventually killed him in a few short years after release. Sadly he met a quick, tragic and early end.

But he never stopped work or stopped dreaming. He never stopped trying to contribute despite his afflictions and bone wearing poverty. The man was obsessed. What we took for a college pick up line, he lived.

So here we have a sly and clever and really funny work some thirty five years ahead of its time. Philip Roth's *The Breast* came around and *Portnoy's Complaint* appeared but 44288 went these two one better and turned a simple one-joke theme into a whole book chock full of word play, absurdities and biting satire. And in so doing pilloried the pomposity of the sexual mores of the decade. Take with me a sheer romp through the newsmakers and people and times of the Seventies with New York landmarks as set. And see once again the people and places that were there.

Marvel at a Class A beautiful mind at play.

We never got to see Vincent Van Gogh pen cartoons for the New Yorker but this is probably the next best thing.

Believe you me, you're gonna laugh hard enough to fall off the sofa.

# Viagro 1

"Something's wrong," Millard Fillmore said.

"Something is terribly wrong."

Millard stood naked in front of his friend, Dr. Harry Wank. He looked embarrassed and disconsolate. He was also standing up and pushing one gross erection directly at the face of his lifelong friend and doctor.

And Dr. Wank, not being in the habit of having erect penises thrust forward at his face, especially by his old and dear friend, Millard, was somewhat taken aback. In fact, he pushed himself all the way back … back flush against the wall.

"Now, Millard…Mill," Dr. Tim Wank pleaded. "Please step the hell away and stop poking air with that damn thing and sit down."

Millard, having realized he had just thrust himself at the face of his friend, and realizing this issue had been settled years ago in junior high school in favor of heterosexuality, flushed with embarrassment and pulled up his jockeys and sat swiftly down. Not, however, down enough to hide this teepee at his crotch for all to see…even, say, by visiting nurses.

Dr. Wank, now having taken full control of his face and somewhat of the situation, relaxed and sat gingerly forward.

"How long have we known each other, Mill?"

"Fifteen years?" Millard asked.

Dr. Wank laughed.

"Yes, about that, now have I ever told you wrong?"

Millard shrugged his shoulders.

"You never told me wrong, Dr. Tim. It's true."

"And when I tell you there's no way one complimentary dose of a little blue pill, even an experimental one, can do this to you and there is nothing, absolutely nothing physically wrong with you to cause it, that's not only true but both a professional and personal opinion."

Millard got up walked over to the front of the desk and whomped his penis down upon the desk. It made a slap and a deep hard thunk sound.

"I think it's growing too," he added.

Once again, Dr. Wank had lost control of the situation. Now his friend was beating his desk with his penis. This was not covered in his Physician's Desk Reference. And Millard's size puzzled him, of course, because the two men had showered together nearly all their young lives, and while not sharing penis measurements per se had always noted each other to be adequately endowed if not right up there near average. But as every woman soon discovers, when these damn things grow, there's no telling where they might stop. But even given that, Tim could not believe the cudgel that thumped his desk so roundly was the same organ with which he had become familiar in his youth. In a quite professional and totally non sexual way, of course. So Dr. Tim girded his buttocks that were barely attached to the chair and prepared to run for his life. To tarry, though, he placed both elbows on the desk.

"I think you can see what's wrong," Millard said and he whacked the desk and once more there was deep resounding thump which caused the door to burst open and a nurse popped her head in and asked if everything was all right.

Dr. Wank assured her all was well and shushed her away and little beads of sweat fell from his forehead.

"You have an erection," Dr. Wank admitted.

"Had it for weeks," Millard said, "ever since you gave me that goddam little blue pill. And that's not all."

"What?" Dr. Wank asked.

Millard drew closer and whispered. "It is growing, swear to God. hell, Tim, you know me, I ain't never been hung like this, even on the best of occasions."

Dr. Wank laughed. He had never seen Mill in the best of his occasions.

"At age forty, Mill, penises stop growing."

Millard grew tense and hunkered up on the desktop so far his chest hung over the edge.

"It's growing, I tell you. I know this."

Once again, the whomp and this time the wood desk vibrated and gave out such a thunk the nurse again rushed in. Dr. Tim smiled and waved her back and the sweat now streamed in little drops off the end of his nose. He'd never been whacked with a penis and he didn't like the prospect of it happening to him just now. Why it might deviate his septum.

Millard peered over the desk to the doctor and waited for a response while the offending little bat waved in air.

Dr. Wank sighed.

"Millard, sit down and take that with you. I tell you everything is OK. There's not a thing wrong to account for this long period of tumescence and to substantiate purported growth. And, by the way, I see no evidence of growth."

Whack, whack, whack went Millard. But he also sat down and looked sad afterwards.

Dr. Wank seriously wondered if his fine wood desk had now been dented.

"Fer gawdsakes!" Millard yelled. "There must be something."

Dr. Wank frowned.

"No, Millard," he said. "What I see is a normal penis in a normal forty year old man, that's all."

"Then why is it growing?"

"It isn't."

"And why does it stay hard all the time?"

"I don't really know," Dr. Wank said. "Perhaps you're going through male menopause. Perhaps this is a psychological reaction. That's pretty common."

Millard skewed his face in anguish.

Dr. Wank continued: "Millard, since there's no physical reason for all this, it has to be in your head. Do you understand? I'd like you to go to a psychiatrist and I have just the right one in mind: Dr. Susan Heatherton. She's a good doctor and I think she can help you. She's doing wonders with menopausal males. Will you go?"

Millard sat back in his chair and sulked. The teepee in his pants twitched as he had graciously pulled up his shorts.

"I'd like to solve this thing here and now, with you," he groused.

Dr. Wank sighed. "I know," Dr. Wank said. "And I would too," he lied. "But there's nothing more I can do besides telling you not to take any more pills and reinterpret tests we've already run which all show nothing."

He reached in the front drawer of his desk and extracted a referral slip which he quickly filled out in script absolutely no one could ever read. And while filling it out, he checked the front of the broad lacquered surface of his desk for dents. It just wouldn't do to have, say, penis forms outlined in wood.

"Dr. Heatherton is good, Millard. You'll like her."

There was this time a courteous and timid knock on the door.

"Come in," Dr. Wank said.

The nurse who kept barging in at every wayward thunk walked into the room. She was young, blonde and buxom and her face looked flushed. She wiggled up to the doctor's desk, smiled easily at Millard and leaned over the doctor's shoulder. There was no way of knowing how much she heard or saw but from the evidence, her curiosity was alarmingly piqued.

"Mrs. Praxell needs her Valium prescription renewed," she cooed. "Would you please sign this?"

Dr. Wank grunted and reached down on the desk for his glasses. The nurse looked up and smiled again at Millard. Millard fidgeted and tried to hide himself but it was largely unsuccessful and the nurse's eyebrows twitched a tad higher upon spying the teepee. The doctor signed the prescription.

"Thank you," said the nurse. She walked to the front of the desk, stopped and looked at her watch. Then she looked at the doctor.

"I know. I'm behind," Dr. Wank said.

She nodded and left the room. Her uniform swished and sighed and before she closed the door she copped this one huge flagrant peek at poor Millard's crotch, sighed mightily, clutched her breast, sucked air, and slammed the door.

"Are we done?" Dr. Wank asked.

He wiped sweat from his nose and face and dearly wanted a drink.

"I guess," Millard replied.

"You will see Susan?"

Millard shrugged.

Dr. Wank rose. Millard stayed seated. He was agitated.

"Dr. Tim, did that nurse do anything sexy?"

"Who, Ellen?"

"Yes."

"No, nothing out of the ordinary." Dr. Wank lied. He'd hired Ellen because her mere presence was sexy. And he dearly wanted Millard out of his office and onto a good psychiatrist's couch. "She is a pretty young thing, though. And she moves well."

"I know," Millard said. "Normal things like that aggravate the hell out of my condition." Millard paused and took a deep breath and stifled a sob. Tears welled in his eyes. "This whole damn thing is driving me nuts. Why'd you give me those damn pills?"

Dr. Wank sat back down and clasped his hands. He tapped his fingertips together and furrowed his brows.

"Susan's our best hope," he said as he blithely ignored the question. He certainly didn't want to tell Millard he was paid by a drug firm to make this trial with this new pill that was being developed as an erection enhancer. And boy was he going to cash that check fast and send this dingbat company back to the drawing board and pronto. Imagine, putting him in this situation. Why they ought to try again thirty years later when they might know something. The decade of the 1970's was not a suitable decade for random and wanton hard-ons, not after the 1960's it wasn't. "You pop on over to her office right now and I'll call ahead and tell her it's an emergency, OK?"

Millard sighed.

"What do I do in the meantime?" Millard asked. Put this damn thing in a box?"

Dr. Wank scowled and reached to a little table beside his chair and pulled out a roll of three-inch tape. He unrolled about a foot and a half of tape and tore the segment off. The tape growled. He handed the piece to Millard.

"Tape that little bastard to your stomach," he said, "and get on the hell out of here and go see Susan."

Dr. Wank wrote an address on the referral slip and handed it to Millard. The miracle was that the address was readable. Millard took the towel off, stood up, turned around and lifted his penis to his stomach and put the tape over it. Surprisingly, it held. Then Millard put on his jockeys and its taut elastic band pulled his penis even tighter and higher against his waist. Millard looked down at himself and noted the offending organ stared up at his chin. Or so he thought.

-It's alive and staring at me, Millard thought. Well, it's sure one big aggravation to me, so Ill call the damn thing aggro like the British aggro for aggravation. And since it seems alive I'll ad a "V" and call it Viagro. Hello, Viagro, ha, like such a stupid thing could really talk. All I got is one aggro to end all Vi-aggros. And so, having had his thoughts duly fuzzed, Millard paid no attention to the fact he'd just personified and named his own penis which is not particularly common in the world of early middle age men. However, should Millard have thought of this as a mental lapse, which it surely was, he would have forgiven it, being as he knew himself to be in a state where it wasn't clear with which head he was truly thinking.

"We're in trouble here," Millard said aloud. "big trouble, Dr. Tim, and we aren't even in River City."

Dr. Wank looked at him and sighed and ignored the reference to "Music Man."

"Maybe. But I tend to think not," he said. "Now, good luck with Susan. And Millard?"

"Yes?"

"Stay the hell away from my nurse."

Millard smiled and Dr. Wank smiled back. Neither man's smile was genuine.

Dr. Wank waved and picked up his phone.

When Millard left the office, Dr. Wank felt so relieved he took a break and slammed down the phone and super quick knocked back two big tumblers of Smirnoff Vodka.

And Millard, when he left, dutifully tried not to look at the nurse. He could feel her staring but he forced himself not to look. He left the waiting room, walked to the hall, got on an elevator, strode through the lobby and passed through the building's outer doors onto Central Park South. There he paused and looked at his referral slip. Dr. Heatherton's office was nearby, just a short walk west. As Millard strolled along Central Park South, he tried to move easily and naturally. This was hard with Viagro taped to his stomach, or so it felt, and the tape pulled hairs out from his stomach and his jerky movements from pain made walking smooth difficult. Millard hiked his pants up so both his pants and belt helped tie his penis to his stomach. The penis head now peeked over the top of his pants and was only covered by his thin shirt. Millard felt exposed, like some flasher. It was as if Viagro were alive and looking up and laughing at him.

"Damn," Millard murmured to himself. He was embarrassed and ashamed. It was being fifteen again, only worse. He was hiding and feeling stupid and grossly self-conscious. Millard ducked into a phone booth as much out of anger and shame as any need to call his office. Once there, he relaxed and punched up his office number.

"Mr. Fillmore's office," came the greeting. Millard flashed a mental picture of his secretary. Jane was pushing thirty, with only fair breasts but a super terrific rump. Millard loved her rump and had for years. He dreamed about her rump. He called for The Claude Zimpfer File at least once a day just to watch Jane wave those two delicious buns in the air. The Zimpfer File was always at the bottom of the file cabinet and she had to stoop to get it.

"Jane, this is Mill. Anything going down?" Millard asked. He winced at his choice of words.

"No," Jane replied. "Mr. Edgar came in to look at the Yiptodd report. Not much else happening."

-Oh, that lousy Edgar, thought Millard. He's also found out how to take a free peek at Jane's buns. Why doesn't he get his own secretary to bend over?

"OK," said Millard. "I'm tied up most of the day, I think, but I'll phone in from time to time. If there's any emergency, hit my beeper, will you?"

-Tied up? Was there no end? And hit my beeper? First it's "going down" and now it's "tied up" and now it's "hit my beeper." Damn, what's next: honk my horn? Why can't I forget my problem?

"Certainly," Jane replied. "I don't look for much to break loose today."

-Break loose? Break loose? Does this woman know I've got a freaking bat strapped to my belly here waiting to break loose and cudgel women and children?

"OK, fine," said Millard. "Be talking to you."

"OK," Jane said. "Bye."

"Bye."

Millard hung up the phone and opened the door of the phone booth. He looked down at his shirt before stepping out and noticed the telltale bulge.

-Wonderful, he thought.

Millard buttoned up his suit coat and strode manfully west. Dr. Heatherton's office was past the Athletic Club, according to the address. Millard negotiated the traffic well and arrived at the building. It was in sight of Columbus Circle and he paused and looked into Central Park before he entered.

-Wonder if I'll wind up in Central Park with the rest of the perverts, he mused.

Millard turned his back on the park and went into the building He checked a directory to find Dr. Heatherton's office. Armed with floor and number, Millard punched the elevator button. When the elevator came, Millard hesitated.

-What am I doing? he asked himself. This is absurd, consulting a psychiatrist about a stupid hard-on.

Millard looked down at his shirt. Viagro wriggled. The visit now seemed only minimally absurd.

Dr. Heatherton's office was plain. There was a small waiting room and a pleasant looking receptionist/nurse was seated behind a glass screen that opened and shut manually. Behind the girl was a file room and from there the suite branched into offices. Millard walked to the screen. The girl looked up and smiled. She had a candy box face and a small mouth. Her upper lip points were high and pronounced and Millard wondered how good she might be at fellatio. Quickly he quashed that thought.

"Hello," Millard said "I'm Millard Fillmore. My doctor just called? I mean recently? From down the street? Dr. Wank?"

"Fillmore? Millard?"

"Yes, anyway, my doctor called and he told me Dr. Heatherton might be able to see me on a semi-emergency basis. He said go right over. Ah, well, so here I am."

"Mil-lard Fill-more?"

"Yes."

The girl fidgeted with some appointment books and other papers and her brow furrowed and relaxed in quick succession. She kept her hand on the glass door and took a deep breath before she spoke.

"Well, Mr. President," she said, "you have a seat in the waiting room and I'll see if the doctor can see you."

"Oh," Millard said. "I'm not the president. It's my true name. Really."

"Of course." The girl smirked and Millard knew right there she didn't believe him.

"Please have a seat," she said, leaving the question of the presidency or its lack thereof totally unresolved.

-Christ, thought Millard, I ought to tell her I'm here to see about a perpetual hard-on. That should make the reason for my visit clear. Millard ground his teeth, went to a chair and sat. The girl walked to one of the offices, knocked, opened a door and leaned in. Her left breast began drawing a sensuous line that surrounded her breast, dipped at her waist, flared at the hip, and trailed languidly down to a well-formed thigh, a pert knee, a high-muscled calf and a trim ankle. The liquid line ended at her toes that pointed out and back ever so gracefully. Viagro stirred, wriggled, throbbed, thumped.

"Down, dammit, down," Millard said. He pulled a magazine up in front of him. He could feel Viagro pulse. The girl nodded her head, broke the line and walked back to the glass screen. She wore a brown, loose and shiny blouse that skittered in folds as her breasts bobbled free. Millard groaned. She sat down, opened the screen and peered out.

"Mr. President, the doctor can see you in a few minutes. You're lucky. We've had an unexpected cancellation."

"Thank you," Millard said.

-For her he'd be president. Millard thought better of telling her of his real problem. It was better now, he decided, to let her think he was President Millard Fillmore.

The girl closed the window and shuffled more papers. Millard hid behind the magazine but as he turned the pages he grew more and more disturbed. It seemed every page had an erotic girl advertising something or other and the glut of pictorial sex rolled Viagro around in the tape. Finally, Millard heard a buzzer and the girl opened the screen.

"You may come in now, Mr. President," she said. She arose and opened a door beside the screen. Millard placed the magazine on the table and checked the buttons on his suit coat. He dreaded a Viagro pop out. He could get arrested. Once inside the file room, Millard followed the girl. He noticed her hips swayed lightly in front of him. The motion pushed him near the edge and was clearly driving Viagro bonkers. Millard bit his lip and hugged his waist to contain himself. The girl opened the office door, smiled and Millard went in. He looked around. In front of him were two chairs and a large and ornate wooden desk. Behind the desk was a woman near his own age. She wore glasses with black strings attached. She removed the glasses in a curt, efficient and professional manner when Millard stepped into the room. Her hair was salt and pepper; her eyes were blue and clear, and she dressed conservatively in a black suit with a small red tie. She was pretty enough to meet Millard's personal criteria of a handsome woman. Behind her were a whole wall full of diplomas and certificates. To the left of the desk, near the wall, was a couch with a chair beside, but placed slightly behind. Millard had never seen the inside of a psychiatrist's office but this particular tableau jibed with his imagination. The woman smiled.

"Hello, Mr. Fillmore," she said. "Won't you sit down?" She smiled even more broadly and gestured to the chairs. Millard sat. "I'm Dr. Heatherton," she continued, "and I've talked with Dr. Wank." She paused and cleared her throat. Millard fidgeted and wondered if the nature of his problem made her as nervous as he. He also wondered how he would tell Dr. Heatherton the details.

-What do I do? he asked. Tell the nice lady I've got a hard-on that doesn't go away and it is growing ... just like that?

Even Millard's thoughts made him blush. Dr. Heatherton waited and smiled. Finally, she broke the silence.

"Well, then, tell me a little about yourself."

She sat back in the chair, pulled a legal pad to her lap and twisted the chair so her body was at a slight angle to the desk.

"I see you're named after a president?"

"Yes," Millard said. "President Millard Fillmore."

"Go on," Dr. Heatherton said.

"Well, when I was born, I'm told, my father took one look at me and decided I would do nothing. So right there he named me after the greatest do nothing president this country ever produced. He said my name would be Millard and he added I also looked lackluster."

"Lackluster?"

"Lackluster. It was his very word. I don't know if I didn't stand out from the other babies in the glass cage or what. Anyway, he thought me lackluster and, since our name already was Fillmore, he called me Millard."

"After the president?"

"Yes, he said President Fillmore was the very standard for being lackluster in presidential history. My father was convinced at first sight I would do nothing and go nowhere and was lackluster he wanted it permanently noted."

"How cruel. How sad for you. Now has your name been a problem to you?"

"Not really. The kids called me Mill and by the time they learned about Millard Fillmore we were in the eighth grade and I was pretty well established."

"Did your name affect your social life or dating?"

"No, I got some razzing in college. Nothing serious."

"Did you have the feeling while growing up your father thought you really lackluster or that you were, in fact, lackluster?"

"Oh, yes, Millard said. "It was apparent right from the first. It was absolutely true. It really was."

"Why?"

"I grew up lackluster, got lackluster grades, took lackluster courses, joined lackluster clubs and did all the lackluster teenage things. The name was accurate, even prophetic. The man was right. We can't fault him from being right," Millard paused. "It's true as an adult and even today," he added.

"What about today?"

"Lackluster."

"Why?"

"I'm an actuary in a large insurance firm. This is probably the premier lackluster job of the mathematically gifted. But I'm chief of the investment section of a pretty fair-sized firm."

"That could be exciting."

"Yes, well, but after you do it a few years, it gets routine and boring."

"Why?"

"Because after you comply with the law, the company policy, the board of directors and such, you have only a few dollars to play with. And those few dollars are usually placed by the company president or the vice presidents."

"So?"

"So anybody can do my job. It takes no thinking, no spirit of adventure. I read the Wall Street Journal to keep current, exercise orders with our brokers on time and in time. And that's it. If I had an idea, and I have had, it's either overruled or there's no money to try it. My job is, like everything else about my whole life is lackluster."

"I see," Dr. Heatherton said. "What about home life?"

"House in the suburbs. One wife named Ethel whom I love dearly. We met in college." Millard paused and smiled. "She is not a great beauty. We have two kids in their teens. They are totally drab. We have no drug problems. There is no hanky panky. No wife swapping. Sex every Wednesday and Sunday although Wednesdays are getting fewer and far between." Millard sighed.

"Lackluster?"

"Quite."

Dr. Heatherton lifted her pencil and leaned back in her chair.

"Let's recap. We have a man in his early forties who is bored with his life and has been as long as he can remember. Is that accurate?"

Millard fidgeted. "Yes. I never thought of it that way. But yes, it's true."

Dr. Heatherton cocked her head and looked over her glasses.

"And I sense this man is bright, sort of romantic, and he thinks life is passing him by. True?"

"Well, partly true." Millard sighed.

"So what does he do?" Dr. Heatherton asked.

"I don't know. What?"

Dr. Heatherton smiles. "He gathers his life force in a simple and demonstrative and dramatic way."

"Oh? Is that so?"

"He gathers his life force into his penis and it stays there, reminding him of his whole drab life and what it could have been. Or, more importantly, what it still might be. This is a wake up call, Millard. You might even say it's a stand up and notice event."

Millard laughed. "Right. But that's ridiculous. It's a hard-on. I could have a tumor on the prostate."

"Is that it?" Dr. Heatherton asked. "And if you did have a tumor, wouldn't your good doctor have found it?

Millard thought.

"He'd have found it," Millard allowed "But it still seems…ah…"

"What?"

"Absurd. And just a little cracked."

Dr. Heatherton stared at Millard.

"No matter," she said after a pause. "This is a preliminary interview and we have only a beginning working hypothesis. I think you might consider your name and how you got it and how it colored your life and expectations. Find out the role your name is playing now, if any.

And you might do well to consider your father and his assessment of you and the effect that has had upon you. Ask, too, what is your role in all this," Dr. Heatherton leaned back in her chair and faced the desk squarely. "Now then, did you ever hear of a self-fulfilling prophecy?"

"Yes."

"Well, that might be part of it. It's worth thinking about." Dr. Heatherton paused. She leaned forward on her desk and Millard noticed her breasts lay softly on the glass top. They folded over the desk lip and rested there like overripe melons. "I offer these things for you to consider," she said seriously and Millard couldn't help wondering if she was speaking of her thoughts or her generous breasts, "but the vital question is what are you going to do here and now about your problem."

"You mean with my hard-on?" Millard blurted.

"Yes." Dr. Heatherton clipped the word short.

Millard sat back in his chair and sighed.

"There's an old joke," Millard said, "about an elderly British gentleman who lived on an estate outside of London. And one morning he got up and his valet started to dress him. 'I say,' said the valet, 'it seems the master sports an erection. Should I notify the mistress of the house?' And the old gentleman looked down at himself and, sure enough, he had a hard-on. 'By George, you're right, Jeeves,' he said. 'What shall we do?' Jeeves asked. The old gentleman thought a while and then a sly smile crossed his face. 'Well,' he said, 'we first shall not tell Madame and second, Jeeves, if you break out my greatcoat, we'll try to smuggle it into London'."

Millard laughed at his own joke.

Dr. Heatherton smiled, only Millard could tell it was a forced smile. Then she waited. The situation turned uncomfortable.

"All right," she said, "so what does that story mean to you?"

Millard shifted in his chair.

-Not much sense of humor, he thought. The lady is all business.

"There's only one place for a hard-on. There's only one real place to put it," he said.

-Actually, there are three places, he corrected himself in his mind.

"I see," Dr. Heatherton said.

Millard squirmed.

"I want to use it but I don't…all at the same time."

"Why? What keeps you from experimenting?"

"Fear," Millard said. "Job, wife and kids are all involved here. Yet it's there…here," he pointed to his crotch, "demanding attention."

"So? Does this disturb you? Do you feel out of control?"

"Yes," Millard said. "Sometimes, I'm near panic."

Dr. Heatherton's eyebrows lifted and then she waited and finally furrowed her brows.

"Interesting," she murmured. "What about this growing phenomenon?" she asked. "Dr. Wank said you think your penis is growing? Isn't that physically impossible?"

"I think it's growing, yes," Millard said.

"You know, of course, mature men's penises do not routinely go on growing?"

"Yes."

"But yours is?"

"Feels like it."

Dr. Heatherton paused and looked down at her desk.

"All right," she said, "let's have a reality check. The first thing I want to do is examine you."

Her teeth clicked shut and her lips tightened.

"Examine?"

"Examine. I want to see this phenomenon and, if true, record it."

"Examine?"

"Examine," said Dr. Heatherton. "I want you to stand up and take off your pants."

She reached in the top drawer of her desk and pulled out a metal ruler. "I'm going to measure your penis each session and we'll keep track of its progress, or lack thereof."

Dr. Heatherton smiled through clenched teeth. Millard could tell she was proposing something that, for her, was unusual and maybe even out of character, perhaps even drastic.

-Oh, God, he thought, I've unsettled a psychiatrist. This can't be good.

"For real?" Millard asked.

"For real," Dr. Heatherton said. Her tone was firm and decided. She stood up, placed her glasses on her nose and strode around the desk, ruler in hand. Millard stood up, unbuttoned his coat, unsnapped his pants and slipped down his shorts. He tore the tape from his belly and the hair it removed caused him to wince and cry out. Viagro dropped from vertical to horizontal and swayed in the air in full erection. Dr. Heatherton's eyes widened. She blanched and gasped and grasped the side of her desk for support.

"What I see," she said, "is a penis in erection."

Millard blushed and looked up to the ceiling.

"Perhaps a tad bigger than normal. And, in truth, well, rather well-formed."

-Migawd, thought Millard, she likes it. She's turned on. What the hell is this?

Dr. Heatherton walked up to Millard, cupped her right hand under the end of his penis and lifted and lowered it until it was exactly horizontal. Millard sighed with pleasure. Dr. Heatherton cleared her throat. Then Dr. Heatherton placed the cold metal ruler on top of Millard's penis. He jumped because the metal on his organ shocked him. But there was the warmth of Dr. Heatherton's hand underneath. Somehow, he felt like a sandwich. Also, it seemed to Millard Dr. Heatherton's hand was just a tad too supportive, a tad too corrective of penis angle during measuring. It was as if she were involuntarily caressing him, giving him a few small strokes, as it were. Dr. Heatherton bent over to look at the ruler more closely.

"Aha," she announced. "You are just certainly normal, perhaps a little on the high side, but definitely normal."

Millard wondered what this scene would look like if the nurse/receptionist happened to walk in on them at this point. How would it appear? Here he was with his pants and shorts down around his ankles, standing, looking at the ceiling and the doctor was fondling his penis in full erection and measuring him with a ruler. How would that look?

"What's that in inches?" Millard asked.

He looked down but the scale of the ruler was too small for him to decipher. Even with bifocals, the centimeter scale was hard to read.

"About seven and three quarter inches," Dr. Heatherton said. "We do not have here a monster."

She stood up briskly, walked back around the desk and sat down where she recorded the measurement on her legal pad. Millard stood with his pants on the floor, his erection waving and his eyes still upon the ceiling. "You may relax," Dr. Heatherton said. Millard looked down at himself. "You may sit down and pull up your pants," she commanded. Millard did as he was told. And, as he did so, he avoided meeting Dr. Heatherton's eyes. Rebinding himself was most difficult. Without the tape, he had to rely on the small elastic band in his shorts and then, when he got on his pants, his belt. But he finally pulled himself up and together.

"Seven and three quarter inches," Millard said aloud, trying to break the tension. "That's bigger than I remember. When I was young one of the guys had a Peter Meter and we all measured ourselves and I was about one size smaller back then."

Dr. Heatherton scribbled on the legal pad and ignored him. Millard continued.

"Yes, ma'm, I recall the official Peter Meter had a tag for each inch or so and do you know what it was for peni between six and seven inches?"

"What?" Dr. Heatherton asked. "Peni is not a word."

Millard could tell she immediately regretted making conversation.

"So it's not the plural of penis? I thought peni was the plural of penis."

"I don't think so."

"Well, seven inches of whatever was called Ladies Home Companion."

"Amusing," Dr. Heatherton replied.

"There was a magazine around at the time with that name."

"Fine," Dr. Heatherton cut him off. "I'd like to see you on a weekly basis. Will that be acceptable?"

"Yes. Sure," said Millard.

He was glad to get back to business. But he noticed Dr. Heatherton's face was flushed and she looked a tad rattled. "Fine," he repeated.

"Is this a good day and time for you?"

"Yes."

Dr. Heatherton arose.

"Well, then, see you next week."

"All right," Millard said. He didn't know whether to say thank you or pleased to meet you or shake her hand or what. In a way, he couldn't bring himself to be formal with a woman who had just grabbed him by the penis, honked his horn as it were, as it seemed all wrong somehow. He didn't know the protocol for this situation. "All right," Millard said. He stood up and started to leave. Before he went through the door, however, he turned to look squarely at Dr. Heatherton. She smiled weird and had this far-a-way look in her eyes.

"Dr. Heatherton?" Millard asked.

"Yes?"

"Thank you for taking me on."

-Oh, shit, thought Millard, here I go again with foot-in-mouth disease.

"I mean for taking me on as a patient." He wondered if Dr. Heatherton also caught that slip.

"That's all right," Dr. Heatherton said. "It was a pleasure." She paused and her browed furrowed as she caught her own foot in mouth reply. "I mean it'll be a pleasure having you...ah, as a patient." She stopped talking right there and rewound her own thoughts. "I mean I think it will be to our mutual advantage to work hard on this problem together."

Millard saw her wince. Even this attempted save was bad. He was now sure she'd caught his slip and had come down with the same foot in mouth disease. Freud would have loved it.

"Yes. Thank you," he said mercifully. "See you next week."

"Fine," she said.

And they both sighed with relief.

Millard walked out of the office and smiled at the girl sitting at the reception desk. She tried to hide her manicuring equipment but it was too late and Millard caught her with her nails up.

"See you next week," Millard said cheerily as he let himself out the door.

-If she types up Dr. Heatherton's notes, Millard thought, she sure won't call me Mr. President again.

"Ah, sure, Mr. President," said the girl.

She seemed flustered and embarrassed. It was a pleasure for Millard to see somebody else in what was now his usual predicament. Millard continued out through the waiting room, pausing only to look at a young man who stared dolefully at him. The young man appeared hostile and disturbed and Millard thought it might be helpful for his own safety if he told the young man he was President Millard Fillmore. But he decided against it. Who knows where disappointed office seekers go to vent their rage, or just where they might spend time?

-This man might believe himself a presidential assassin, Millard thought.

So Millard traveled quickly out of the room and out into the hallway. He walked to the elevator, punched the button and waited. Once in the elevator, Millard found himself alone and he hummed to himself. He had a problem, sure, but he was doing something about it, taking all the right steps. It wasn't so bad.

The elevator stopped the next floor down and the door opened on a crowd of people who scurried to jump on. Millard was pushed to the back corner and a small woman stood up against him. She was no taller than his chest and Millard panicked momentarily because Viagro bulged out at her at chest level. Millard was relieved when she smiled at him and turned around to face the front. She had a full mouth and pretty features and rich black hair and a nice figure. There also was about her a hint of perfume. The people kept piling in and the woman pressed back harder and harder until there was no escaping the fact Viagro was inserted directly and firmly in the hollow of her back between her shoulder blades. Millard sweated and waited for the woman to react. But she didn't. Well, not at first. She waited and then looked up and around at Millard in amazement. She stared at him and then smiled evilly out of one side of her mouth.

"Enough, enough," shouted two men from the back as more people tried to cram into the little box. And the crowding stopped while the doors clacked in a futile attempt to close. The front line of the people in the elevator undulated as the doors moved closer and closer together and some scooted back harder and, finally, some got off. At length, the doors closed and this stuffed cell of humanity sighed collectively and waited. The tiny woman in front of Millard leaned back and moved her shoulder blades back and forth while she, herself, moved up and down experimentally. Millard couldn't help himself. He groaned and sighed. She turned.

"Am I hurting you?" she asked in a loud and pleasant voice. She smirked. Millard could tell she was totally aware of his problem.

"No, it's all right," he said.

The woman turned around and to Millard's surprise she nestled her shoulder blades around Viagro and enveloped it like some greedy womb. A buzzer sounded and the elevator refused to move.

"Too many," called one of the men from the back. He and his friend seemed to know all about the elevator. Millard got the impression this was an entire office moving and that they shifted floors frequently.

"Push the Open Door button," Mr. Know All Elevator Man commanded. Soon, the doors opened and three persons from the front stepped off. The pressure was relieved but the little woman in front of Millard moved back instead of forward. She pressed even harder against him. Only now she worked her shoulders back and forth rhythmically from side to side and was also bobbing up and down.

-Migawd, thought Millard, what'll I do? I'm getting a hand job in public…only it's more than a simple hand job, it's a whole body job.

He wanted to shift or run but the crush of people held him firm. The woman increased her actions side to side and up and down. It was maddening and it shattered Millard's former complacency about his potential for handling his problem.

-Damn, he thought and then he thought, well, hell, it is New York so just relax and enjoy it.

The elevator stopped at the next floor and the doors opened to reveal another group of people as large as the first. This once again produced a collective moan as the elevator occupants saw another huge crowd in front of them. The people in the elevator laughed and waved and hooted and somebody joyfully farted. The woman used the opportunity to increase her back and body action on Viagro and Millard went quietly mad. Then he felt hands on his thighs and these hands cleverly slipped between his legs and tickled his scrotum.

"Excuse me," Millard said. The woman turned and looked up at him. Her face was pure innocence, even though her eyes were glazed and there was an idiotic slanted smile on her face, as if she'd left her vibrator on high and fallen asleep.

"Yes?" she asked.

"I was wondering if you had enough room. Are you certain you're comfortable?"

"Yes, I'm fine," she answered. "Just fine. Thank you so much for asking."

She turned and inhaled deeply and then viciously scrunched her shoulders together. The squeeze nearly popped Millard's already swollen member but it also was extremely pleasurable and Millard felt a huge, wet, scream-loud climax was not far away. The woman then bobbed up and down so much and so vigorously Millard was sure the rest of the occupants of the elevator knew exactly what was happening.

Then the elevator stopped and just as suddenly as the crush entered it departed. The woman waited for the other people to file off and then she stepped forward, stopped the doors from closing and looked full at Millard who was now alone and slumped in the corner and in somewhat of a physical agony.

"You pervert," she shouted and slapped his cheek with a resounding thwack. "And thanks," she said.

The doors closed and Millard's eyes watered from the sting and his cheeks burned. He looked up and around and in surprise.

"Oh?" said Millard to the closed doors. He was baffled.

Suddenly, the doors snapped open and the woman reappeared and her face was flushed and features contorted and her mouth twisted in fury.

"You pervert," she hissed again and the doors snapped shut before she could slap him again..

Millard arrived at the lobby alone and was so slow in getting off he almost got thrown back by all the new people getting on.

-What the hell happened there? he asked.

Millard made his way to the street. His eyes teared, his face was crimson and he walked wobbly and he felt confused, humiliated and weak.

And, also, his balls ached with a severe case of Lovers' Nuts plus he felt almost terminally horny.

# Viagro 2

Millard walked to Columbus Circle. The air somewhat revived him. He told himself what happened was merely an aberration of urban life. Naturally, he concluded, the woman was demented. What else? But then, he reminded himself, he also was demented. Even though he was seeing about it and had his very own doctor and was working-on-the-problem, he was still demented. Millard smiled to himself. It was good to say he was working-on-the-problem. It sounded decisive. Millard crossed Central Park West after looping the northeast arc of Columbus Circle. He continued north on Central Park West and beside him, on his right, was Central Park. It was pleasant to look into the greenery, so much so that Millard sat on a bench by the park wall and stared into the park. Then he turned to stare into the lobby of the Mayflower Hotel and sorted his thoughts about the incident.

-It's all crazy, he decided. Perhaps we both are. Anyway, it's not worth worrying about. No, it's certainly not worth worrying about.

Millard looked at his watch. It was still early so he decided to visit the West Side "Y" and see if he could pick up a handball game. It'd be good to exercise, he thought, and with that in mind he arose and walked to Sixty Third Street, crossed Central Park West and strode briskly to the "Y." Once inside, he thought he'd better call the office again. He walked through the entrance, then the lobby, to a bank of phones. He dialed his office and checked in with Jane. Her silky voice soothed him but there was nothing much happening. Millard replaced the phone on the hook and went upstairs to the Business Men's Club. He checked in and went to his locker. Once there, he started to undress. As he unbuttoned his shirt, a terrible thought struck him: what was he going to do with the hard-on? Millard looked around. A group of men were replaying a racquetball game. They stood nearby in various states of undress and were concerned only with the game. Yet Millard was near panic because he could picture their reactions if he took his pants down and stood there naked with a hard-on. This wasn't the Luxor Baths where a hard-on was required; this was the nice, respectable West Side "Y." And a hard-on would stand out. Millard chuckled at the phrase "stand out" and noted the double entendre.

-Maybe I'll just shower, Millard thought to himself.

But that was impossible, as was the sauna, the swimming pool, the weight room and the steam bath. The masseur was out of the question. In fact, there was no place in the "Y" he could go with a hard-on with the possible exception of some resident Mary Poppit's room upstairs. While Millard pondered the dilemma, Binky Derth came up and slapped him on the back.

"Hi, Mill," he said. He sat down beside Millard and puffed heavily. In his hand he held a racquet and some balls. His sweatshirt was soaked and his hair, quite askew, was held somewhat in check by an elastic band. "What's happening?" he asked.

"Nothing," Millard replied.

Binky looked him over. Millard had taken off his suit coat and unbuttoned the top of his shirt. That was it.

"You coming or going?" Binky asked.

-Jesus, this guy is a bore, Millard thought.

Binky also worked in insurance but for a competing company. And he was a salesman. But worse than that, he was a chronic promoter.

"Going," Millard said. "I'm going."

"Did you work out?" Binky asked.

"No."

"Well, shit, Mill," Binky said, "at least take a steam or hit the sauna." He patted Millard's leg. "We all feel like hell now and then." Binky smiled and stood up and slipped off his gym clothes. He opened his locker and threw in the sweats and pulled out a clean white towel. He wrapped the towel around his hips and slipped into a pair of rubber sandals. He looked down at Millard who was fiddling with his tie. "A shower maybe?"

"No, thanks," said Millard. He could see himself in a towel with his hard-on poking out and drawing censorious stares. "No thanks," he repeated. "I'm a little under the weather."

"Hey," Binky said, "that's too bad." He sat down. "You OK? Anything I can do?"

Millard sighed. Binky had all the right words but Millard knew him to be a total fake and not really interested. Binky was a rat, a throat-cutting, commission-hunting rat.

"See, look, Bink, I got this problem," Millard whispered, "which is really terrible." He looked around conspiratorially.

"Oh?"

"I got this hard-on, see? And it won't go away. It stays up for hours and hours and won't go away. And I think it's there forever, know what I mean? And, well, to tell the truth, carrying around a burden like that, I mean, hey, I'm exhausted." Millard looked as sincere as he could. He then dropped his eyes and wagged his head for emphasis. Telling the truth here was just bizarre enough to send Binky packing.

"Ha?!" Binky exclaimed. "That true?"

"Oh, yes," said Millard. "It's true."

Binky jumped up laughing. "Gawddam," he said, "that's the funniest thing I've heard today. It should be in 'The Times.' I can see it now: 'Man Sidelined by Hard-on at West Side "Y"; Jock Exhausted After Carrying Around A Heavy Erection. Racquetball Game Severely Curtailed.' That's great. You're a card, Mill. A real card."

Binky got up and headed for the sauna. His sandals slapped on the floor and he laughed and chuckled to himself. "That's great. Woo-ee! That's funny. Ha!"

Millard buttoned up his shirt collar, stood, put on his coat and left. He was proud as could be.

-The best way to handle people like Binky Derth is to tell the truth, Millard thought, because when they do hear it, they never believe it and they leave you alone.

Once on the street, Millard walked west to O'Neill's Balloon. O'Neill's was right next to the Empire Hotel. The bar got its name in the distant past when it was illegal to call a saloon a saloon. O'Neill called his place a balloon and the name stuck. Future owners became superstitious about this odd name and refused to change it. At least that was the story. Millard liked O'Neill's. They had a great chocolate mousse. Also, it was across from Lincoln Center and Millard liked to gaze at the fountain and the plaza. Show folk frequented the balloon and it wasn't infrequent to see a TV soap actor sitting at a table along with an occasional legitimate theater actor. Millard crossed Broadway, sidled past the lobby of The Empire and strode into O'Neill's. The mural on the south wall amused him once again. It was a backstage scene of some long-forgotten show. The actors were life size and staring forward and out into the bar. They perched on stage scenery and stools and other paraphernalia. The actors' faces were portraits, no question, but they also could serve as show biz archetypes. They had a classic brazen vulnerability. Millard found the mural both enchanting and haunting.

"Party of one?" the maitre'd asked. He was young and pretty like all the waiters and waitresses. Millard thought O'Neill's must be staffed with unemployed actors, either that or students from Fordham University which was only a block away.

"Yes. One. May I have a window table?"

"Sure."

The maitre'd led Millard to the northwest corner of the balloon and seated him. It was perfect. Millard had a view down Columbus Avenue and up to where Broadway met Columbus. He could see Lincoln Center and the fountain and the triangular traffic island in front of the Empire. It was a good view and Millard was pleased. If he stretched, he could see Fordham's grounds. He noticed they recently added some sculptures.

Millard had always been interested in the arts, oh, not enough to do anything, but interested. He wondered about art even as a young man as he ploughed through college with courses such as economics, accounting, marketing and statistics. Even then, he envied the fine arts majors. Occasionally, as a student, he'd sit in front of his ledgers and calculator and wonder what it would be like to paint or sculpt or act. But it never happened.

"Hi, I'm your waiter, Bruce."

"Oh?" said Millard. "Of course you are."

"You ready to order?"

"Yes, the chocolate mousse."

"Anything to drink?"

"Ice tea. No. Make that bourbon and water…a double."

Bruce winced. Millard knew mousse and bourbon was not a really good combination. But what the hell, he wanted both. The waiter was too sensitive.

-Most artsy people are sensitive, Millard reminded himself. So I scratched his sensitivity. Sue me.

The chocolate mousse was not long in coming. Neither was the drink. Millard bolted the drink and ordered another. While Bruce was away, Millard dug into his mousse.

-Ah, he said to himself, that's great.

About midway through, Bruce returned and set the second drink down. Millard looked up and caught Bruce in the act of wrinkling his nose. Unfazed, Millard continued. Then he bolted the second drink and ordered a third. Millard was feeling content when his meal was interrupted.

"Hi," Binky Derth said. He sat down.

-Sumbitch, Millard thought, not even a by your leave or a do-you-mind.

"Hi," Millard said.

Binky tossed an attache case into a chair.

"I been thinking," Binky said, "about this hard-on thing."

"Oh?"

-Oh, God, was what Millard really thought.

"Yeah. And the way I see it, there's money in it. Big money."

"Good."

"First off, if you could find out what's causing it and put it in a pill you could sell it. I know about ten million guys who'd pay big for a guaranteed hard-on. And that's just statewide. Worldwide, it'd be bigger. China's a fantastic market for that stuff. Second, you yourself could become a celebrity. Why we could book you on talk shows, Merv and Johnnie come to mind, and we could have the National Enquirer do a piece on you. Then we can do a book. Then we could get a movie made from the book. And also, Mill, you could do promo stunts like, well, taking on a hundred girls in one night…sort of a sexual stunt man. And maybe get you to do guest shots in porn movies, I mean the money will just roll. Probably the receipts from your 'Magic Little Viagro Blue Pill' sales will make you a billionaire. Can't you see it, Mill? See your name in lights? Listen, stick with me here, I'm going to make you a star."

"Where have I heard that?" Millard said. He was amused. And it all happened in O'Neill's of all places. It was typical because Binky thought about making money and promoting just about everything.

"Two words: Colonel Tom Parker.'

"That's three words. Who?"

"Parker. The guy behind Elvis."

"I knew there had to be somebody behind. Those hips couldn't move like that without some support."

"Sure. Colonel Tom. A great man. Anyway, if you're the first man alive with a perpetual hard-on, we can sell it. We can cash it out; we really can."

"What if I don't?"

Binky's face fell.

"Don't? Don't? Who would do a don't on this? If you did do a don't on this then you just passed up a bazillion dollars and our deal is off," Binky said. "Yessir, the deal is off." He grew quiet and despondent. "Imagine a person who would do a don't on this great little moneymaker."

"I lied," Millard said. "There's no perpetual hard-on. It was an excuse not to work out."

Binky sighed.

"I knew it. I knew it was too good to be true," Binky said. "But the possibilities of such a happening, Jesus, the possibilities are enormous. Can't you see that, Mill? I couldn't help thinking about it. A thing like that…wow! The money to be made… well, it's just incredible. Wow!" Binky wagged his head.

"I'll bet."

"Enormous potential. Absolutely enormous. But, well, I'd never run into a bonanza like that."

"Bonanza or banana?"

"What?"

"Did you say 'bonanza' or 'banana'?"

Binky shrugged. "Why would I say banana? It doesn't matter, does it? When it isn't so?"

"Of course not," Millard replied. "Some people like bananas."

"Right. So there you are."

Binky sat for a while and Millard watched the death of dreams. It wasn't a pretty sight. But on Binky it looked good.

"I'd like to see it through," he said. "I'd really like to see it. I could handle it; I really could."

"Handle? You want to handle it? You do, Binky? I'm surprised. I didn't know you handled things like that; I didn't know you were that way."

"Yes. I mean no. I mean you know what I mean."

"Sure. Just kidding."

"Well, don't. Don't fun with that kind of stuff. The pun is the lowest form of humor you know."

"Was that a pun? Did I say pun? Didn't I really say fun, Binky?"

"I don't know. Just stop it." Binky sighed, "Stop it!" He got up and grabbed his attache case. "Be seeing you, Mill," he said. "It was nice to think about."

"Oh, so now you admit you think about it?"

"Stop it!"

"Sure," Millard said, "But I really didn't know you thought about it."

"A bazillion dollars, a bazillion dollars, aren't you listening? That's always something to think about. That's what I think about."

"Yes. Of course it is. What was I thinking? Sure. That's it. Yes. For sure."

"You bastard. Yeah, well, I'll keep my eyes open. If I find someone with that condition, I'll tell you and we'll go partners."

"Good. That's great. Everybody needs a partner," Millard said, "especially if one handles those sorts of things and thinks about it a lot."

Millard could see fury in Binky's eyes. But Binky walked away from the table and stayed silent. Millard smiled to himself and ordered another drink. He dawdled with it, looked at the view, and then, reluctantly, finished. Millard waved Bruce over.

"Yes?"

"Check."

"Certainly." Bruce smiled.

-These sensitive waiter types always smile at check time, Millard told himself.

Bruce totaled the bill and laid it on the table. Millard checked the check and reached in his pocket for a tip. He left ten percent.

-He doesn't deserve more, Millard thought, after all that wincing disapproving glances. Who's he to judge if a person wants bourbon with mousse?

Pleased with his vengeance, Millard got up and went to the rest room. It was small; it had two urinals and one john. One of the urinals was occupied. Millard stepped up and unzipped his pants. Then it hit him: what would the man next to him think if he whipped out one fully erect penis? Would he get in trouble? Worse yet, would he get admiring glances and get propositioned? You can never tell with actors. What? Millard fumbled at his pants to kill time. It was no use; the man next to him seemed afflicted with bashful kidneys. Or he was fishing, one or the other. Millard looked around at the john.

-I'll pretend I've noticed another urge here, Millard thought, and get in the john where it's private.

No dice. The john was occupied. A pair of Gucci shoes with gray pants rumpled and sacked around them peeked out at him from under the door. Millard cleared his throat and walked out as if the urge to urinate had been a false alarm. He stepped to the cash register, paid his tab and left. It suddenly dawned on him that by and large he could never piss in a public rest room, at least not without a john.

-Holy hell, Millard said to himself. First I'm prevented from using the "Y" and now this.

He sat down on the Broadway side of the Empire Hotel traffic island and waited for a downtown bus. The pressure on his kidneys was terrible but the pressure on his mind was even worse.

At the office, Jane greeted Millard with a pleasant smile and a sheaf of phone messages she thrust into his hand.

"You OK?" she asked.

"Sure," Millard said. "Went to the 'Y' and ate a late lunch at O'Neill's."

"You had the mousse again?"

"Yes."

She harrumphed. He always had the mousse. Millard checked the messages. Most were routine; few needed answering. But Millard felt dutiful after what was for him a long absence from the office. So he went into his office and punched up number after number. Most of the men he called were out and Millard left messages. "Tell him Millard Fillmore called," he said. The routine took the better part of a half an hour and when it was over Millard was satisfied the ball was now in the other court. Now they'd have to call him. Phone tag was sport to him.

-That's the way business works, he told himself. We play phone games.

Millard leaned back in his chair and reached for his Wall Street Journal. There he checked out the prime interest rate. It was the only statistic he needed when he dealt with other company executives. It wasn't the only one he needed when he was placing orders. But it sure was the one he needed to look "current" and "aware." Millard tossed the paper aside with disgust. The prime rate quote was also a game to him, a needless statistic with which he played the alert employee game with his bosses.

Millard sighed and opened the desk drawer and checked his chart. On the chart were current investments plotted against time. It was an original chart devised by Millard to keep track of what-was-where and what-needed-to-be-done and when. He'd fancied it up over the years so he could also keep track of his fantasy investments: the ones disallowed or overruled. Millard chuckled to see his "wish" list outperforming the actual list by huge margins. Millard checked one severe valley that was the brainchild of the company president. Who the hell bought toothpicks? What a dork. He wondered how he was going to cover that in a report so neither he nor the president would look foolish. It was a problem both familiar and ongoing. But it was less of a problem than reporting back to the board of directors when their choices bombed, which they did with regularity.

Millard set the chart aside and put his hands behind his head and stared at the ceiling. He was acutely aware of Viagro and he felt it push against his belt and shirt. He looked down and stared back at the single eye that stared back at him through the membrane of his cotton shirt. It was scary. Viagro seemed more and more alive; he seemed distinct and living a life of his own, as if Viagro was becoming a separate entity. Jane walked into the office and sat in front of Millard. Viagro wriggled.

"We going to execute some Ginny Maes tomorrow?" she asked.

"Dunno," Millard said. "I think I'll get board approval for that, at least for the amount we've planned."

Millard stared at Jane. She was pretty in a special way and she'd been with him a long time. She served him well and was both efficient and proficient. They'd never been close, always professional. Viagro twisted and Millard felt compelled to introduce a new element into his relationship with Jane. Oh, he'd thought of it before, but this time the urge was more insistent, more demanding. It was as if the action were dictated.

"Jane," Millard said, "do you know why I ask you for the Zimpfer file so often?"

"Because you want to check something?"

"Partly."

"Oh. Well, why then?"

Millard leaned forward in his chair. He wanted to strike the right note here.

-Don't scare her off, he warned himself. Go easy.

"Because," Millard said, "I have ulterior motives."

Jane giggled. Millard could see she was relaxed and calm and not threatened at all.

"Why don't you get it for me now and bring it here and we'll talk."

"Sure," Jane said. When she got out of the chair, her breasts pointed up and forward and out. This sight rolled Viagro and Millard thought he heard a groan. Jane turned and walked to the bank of file cabinets, found the set she was looking for and bent down. Millard filled his eyes with the generous bottom waving in the air. Jane retrieved the file, stood up and walked back to the desk. She placed the file in front of Millard. Her face was flushed.

"Sit down," Millard said. He patted the file. Jane brushed a lock of hair from her forehead and sat. She looked expectant. Millard patted the file. "Claude Zimpfer was a double indemnity case. He's been dead for seven years. The account has been paid; the check cashed and for all I know the widow is living in the south of France."

"Oh?" Jane said.

"It's a dead file, Jane. I keep it for one reason and one reason only."

"And why's that?"

"Because Claude Zimpfer has a last name beginning with 'Z'."

"So?"

"So when I ask to see it, it's not the file I want to see, it's you."

Jane frowned.

-Careful, Millard warned himself, be very careful.

"Me?"

"You." Millard looked squarely into Jane's eyes. "I find you attractive." Jane blushed and averted her eyes.

"Ah, well," she said, "thank you. But I don't see what all this has to do with the dead Mr. Zimpfer."

Millard sighed and looked to the ceiling. Viagro thrashed its bonds.

"I like to watch you get the Zimpfer file because I like to see you move," Millard said.

"Is that all?" Jane asked. "So what's wrong with my moving?"

"Nothing. I like to see it, that's all."

Silence grew. Millard waited. Jane waited. Millard watched waves of awareness wash over Jane's face. None seemed to disturb her; they seemed to come and go regularly, breaking on an even temperament.

"Mr. Fillmore?"

"Yes?"

"Do you think I'm a good secretary?"

"Yes. The best."

Jane smiled. She looked aware and, suddenly, clever.

"Don't you think," she said, "I know all about Claude Zimpfer and what's in his file or what isn't in it?"

"Well, yes," Millard admitted, "I guess that'd have to be true."

"Count on it," Jane said. "I'm good at what I do."

"And?"

"And I am well aware of Mr. Zimpfer's deadness. So if I get a dead file for you for years and there's no change in it, no reason for it, at least file-wise, don't you think I might have wondered what might be the real reason?"

"Have you?"

"Of course." Jane smiled and waited. She leaned back in the chair and stroked her pencil.

=Now! Viagro shouted. Now's the time. Tell her you've watched her buns for all these years and grown fond of her. Do it now! She's waiting! Ask her to dinner! Do something. Anything! Whip the desktop clean and throw her down and pork that little honey right on the desk!

Millard was stunned. Viagro talked! It wasn't out loud but there was this clear voice in his head, a definite voice all low and gravelly and crude. Jane leaned forward.

"I get the Zimpfer file because I like to move for you, Millard," she said.

"Thank you," Millard blurted. "I wanted you to know." Millard was distracted by Viagro's voice. He was also uncomfortable with Jane's response because she seemed too eager and too accepting.

"I wanted you to know I knew," Jane purred.

=Ball her on the desk, right there over the Zimpfer file. Or in the chair. Get it on! Viagro urged.

"Thank you," Millard said.

=Thank you? You're saying "thank you"? What the hell is this? Viagro shouted.

"Thank you," Jane said.

Millard tried desperately to silence Viagro. He felt like he was flying apart inside and that he was chasing down separate parts of him. Jane, noting the hesitation, arose and picked up the file from the desk and walked back to the cabinets. To Millard's inner turmoil was added the sight of Jane's moving. Millard thought she walked more slowly, that her hips swayed more provocatively and she bent over more seductively. And once her buns were in the air, they moved more temptingly. Viagro groaned and roared so loud Millard was sure Jane could hear him. But Jane walked back to the desk.

"Will that be all?" she asked.

"For now," Millard said.

"Fine," Jane said. "I'll be glad to get the Zimpfer file any time you need to look at it."

Millard managed to smile. "I may be needing it frequently in the near future." Millard panicked a little. Was that his voice? Or was it partly Viagro?"

Jane exhaled.

"Fine," she said "because I happen to know I've got the finest butt on either side of the Hudson and I'm damn proud of it and a girl needs to air a thing like that every once in a while." And with that she left the office and closed the door quietly behind her.

=What are we doing here? Viagro asked. The woman was ready and, from all appearances, has been for years.

-Sure, OK, Millard replied. Take it easy.

=Easy? Why take it easy? You're ready; she's ready. It's that simple.

-I am taking it easy, you understand?

=No. You're just a coward; that's what you are. A coward!

-Get off it.

=I won't. Secretaries are fair game. I'm tired of standing around and doing nothing.

-Who asked you? Millard said firmly. Who asked you to stand around?

=Don't play dumb with me. You know. You just won't admit it to yourself. Your father was right. You are one lackluster sumbitch you are.

-Leave my father out of it.

=I'm trying.

-Do it.

=Look, Viagro said, you're not telling me anything. Hear that? From now on, I'm telling you. Little head tells big head. Like that.

-Is that so?

=That's so.

Millard got up from his desk and walked to the coffee pot. He was unnerved.

-What the hell is this? he asked. I'm talking to my own penis that is talking back and now it's threatening me. This is crazy.

Millard grasped the coffee stand to steady himself and then poured a cup of coffee. His hands shook and he felt a light cold sweat on his brow.

-Perhaps, he thought, I need Dr. Heatherton more than I imagined.

He gulped the coffee and burned his mouth.

"Sheesh!" he exclaimed.

Millard walked over and sat down at his desk. He was afraid to go out of the office, afraid to confront Jane. He also was afraid to meet any of his fellow executives. His mind was awash in fear. He felt Viagro as a living presence that had developed a mind of its own. The "talking" was most distressing, that and his acting on his own worst impulses. Millard felt out-of-control, no longer the master of himself. Viagro was taking over, moving into his thoughts and dictating his deeds. It was bad enough when it first started, when there was just a constant hard-on. And it was worse when he felt Viagro to be growing as he had earlier in the day. All that was bad enough. But now, with Viagro alive and threatening, it was absolutely terrible. Millard looked at his watch. He could leave if he wished. It was late enough, early for him, but late enough. Millard got up and stretched. He took a few deep breaths to calm himself. As he stretched, Viagro strained against the cloth and elastic bonds.

=Hey! Viagro called, where we going?

-Migawd, Millard thought. He won't shut up.

Millard bolted from the office and stood disheveled and breathless before Jane's desk.

"Jane?"

"Yes?" She smiled warmly. Then the smile waned and a look of concern crossed her face. You OK?"

"No. I mean yes. I mean yes and no." Jane waited. Millard continued. "I'm not feeling too well and I think I'll leave early. Nothing serious. But I'd like to get a head start on the weekend."

"OK, That's fine," Jane said. "Anything I can do?"

=Whoa! Viagro groaned. Damn straight. That's an invitation.

"No, I think not," Millard replied as he ignored Viagro. "Thanks."

Millard felt the ghost of Claude Zimpfer in the air. It hung like a presence around him and popped up behind the words he was saying and the words Jane used to answer.

=Mention the file. Mention dinner. Mention a hotel, Viagro growled.

-No, Millard answered defiantly.

"Well, see you Monday," Jane said.

"Sure," Millard said. He forced a smile and left. He saw Jane as relaxed and that reassured him. He still could not pound down a sense of foreboding because he knew Jane was patient, like a spider in a web, but her patience now gave him time to find a way to cope. That and the weekend. Millard looked forward to the weekend. There wasn't much standing between him and the weekend, just a couple of drinks, a short ride on the commuter, a small drive from the station and home. Millard left the building and his spirits lightened. For the first time today, he knew where he was going and what he was going to do. It was refreshing.

Once home, the force of the day's events lessened and Millard found a measure of peace. Ethel was abuzz with suburban gossip and, even though Millard knew none of the principals, he listened with interest. The kids disrupted the dinner only by eating quickly and noisily and then leaving. Millard found himself in the kitchen after dinner with his wife.

"We have anything on this weekend?" he asked.

"No. Not much," Ethel answered.

"Good," Millard said, "I'd like a quiet time, sort of a mini-vacation at home."

"Oh?" Ethel looked up from packing the dishwasher and stared at Millard." Anything wrong?'

"No," Millard replied, "I'd just like a little peace and quiet over the next two days. I need to regroup."

Ethel walked over the kitchen table and sat down. She frowned and tears welled up in the corners of her eyes. Millard caught his mistake. He'd said he'd needed peace and quiet. That implied he didn't get those qualities and therefore, to Ethel, he'd said the house was not a refuge but an irritant. Second, he'd said he wanted to regroup. That meant to Ethel he needed to regroup from the household and whatever else was bothering him.

-I'm an old married man, Millard thought. I shouldn't be making stupid newlywed mistakes.

"It's the hard-on, isn't it?" Ethel asked.

"What?" Millard was amazed. He thought he was in for a long and rough domestic discussion in which he'd have to soothe Ethel's feelings.

"It's the hard-on, isn't it?" Ethel repeated the question. She leaned back in the chair and placed her hands behind her head and cocked her right leg over the left. "I guess we ought to talk about it, lord knows it's been going on long enough."

"What hard-on?" Millard asked. He sat opposite Ethel at the kitchen table.

"Don't what hard-on me. The one you've been carrying around for weeks."

"You know?"

"Sure I know. God, Millard, we met in college. If there's one course in college all girls master it's Hard-on Detection 101. Christ, we've been studying since the sixth grade. I know."

"Well, I went to the doctor today," Millard admitted.

"And?"

"And he said there was nothing wrong."

"Good."

"…Physically."

"Oh, shit!"

"So he recommended a psychiatrist."

"Migawd."

"And I went to see her."

"Her?"

"Her."

"For a hard-on problem?"

"Yes."

"And?"

=And she took out a Peter Meter and measured me, Viagro said.

-Shut up! Millard commanded.

"And we…ah…started therapy."

=With a goddam ruler we did. It was great.

Ethel arose and went over to the kitchen stove. She put some water on to boil and laid out two coffee cups with saucers into which she spooned some instant coffee. When the water steamed, she poured the water into the cups and sat back down.

"What did your doctor say?"

"Not much. She asked me to think about my name and why my father gave it to me and what it's done and what he's done and what I've done about the lackluster thing."

=And the Peter Meter. Don't forget that! She made a sandwich.

-Shut up!

"Hell, I could have done that," Ethel said. "You and a book on basic Freud could have done that."

"I know. But it's a start."

"She good?"

=She strokes nice.

"Comes highly recommended."

"But were you impressed?"

"Not impressed. But she's supposed to be good with male menopause. It was only a first session."

Ethel's cup clattered on her saucer.

"Migawd," she said. "I'll bet you got some young chippie on the side?"

"No."

"On your mind then?"

"No."

=Hey Turkey, tell her about Claude Zimpfer.

"What, then?"

"What do you mean, what?"

"Oh, hell, I don't know." Ethel looked down solemnly at her coffee. She picked up her spoon and dawdled. "It's just not all that comfortable watching your husband walk around for weeks with a hard-on and then having him tell you he's under psychiatric care."

"I know," Millard said, "but I'm working on it. I'm doing something about it. Working-on-the-problem."

Ethel burst into tears.

"Why didn't you tell me?"

"I didn't want to worry you. I thought it was just a temporary thing. That it'd go away. I didn't want to worry you."

Ethel cried quietly to herself. Millard got up and stood beside her and cradled her head against his stomach. He patted her back and stroked her temple.

"It's OK. It's going to be OK," he said.

Ethel looked up at him.

"Promise?" she asked.

"Promise," Millard said. Inside, however, he felt less than sure.

That evening in bed, Ethel asked for reassurance physically by turning her back and then scooting close to Millard so they lay together like two spoons in a drawer. Millard nuzzled Ethel and she moved her head slightly to acknowledge him. Millard felt warm and tender, emotions that, before his problem, led directly to making love. But now he felt faintly obscene because he was always ready. There was no build up, no progression of tenderness, no feeling of turning passion into love. Viagro robbed him of that. So they lay together, hugging and nuzzling and chaste.

By Sunday afternoon, Millard and Ethel had become nervous in each other's presence. There was a wall between them, a wall of silence, anger, hurt and resentment. Millard felt for the first time not at home in his own house. He wanted to leave but there was no place to go. And he felt Ethel wanted him to leave but didn't want to be alone. There was an argument Sunday evening.

"Do you want hamburgers for dinner?" Ethel asked.

"That'd be fine," Millard answered.

"We have chicken. I could fry some chicken."

"That'd be fine, too."

"Well, which do you want?"

"Either is OK. What do you want?"

"There's cold cuts. We could have cold cuts and soup."

"Cold cuts sounds nice."

"Then you want cold cuts?"

"I want whatever you want."

Ethel fidgeted and fumed.

"Look," she said "I'm asking for a decision. I've given you three damn choices."

Millard was taken aback by the sharpness of her tone. But as an old married man, he knew what was in store.

"It doesn't make any difference. I want what you want. That's all."

"No. I asked you!"

"OK, I like hamburgers. Let's have hamburgers. Hamburgers are nice. Do hamburgers."

Ethel frowned.

"The chicken's been frozen for a long time. If we don't use it soon, it'll go bad."

"Well, have the chicken then. I like hamburgers but if the chicken's going to spoil, let's have the chicken."

"You're so difficult. You never make a decision. Our whole life is like that! You never make a decision. I can't take this any more."

"Have the cold cuts, then. I don't care. C'mon now…" Millard pleaded but he knew that never worked.

"No. It's true. You're wishy-washy. Gutless. Lackluster is what you are."

"Fer gawdsakes, Ethel, what is this?"

"I ask you a simple question and you sit there and say 'yes' to everything."

"Hamburgers!"

"Sure, first it was hamburgers, then it was chicken, then it was cold cuts."

"Honey, let's go out. Can we go out? I'll buy."

"What?"

"Let's go out to eat. I'll take us out."

"Where?"

"I don't know. What are you hungry for?"

"Oh! Oh! You're doing it again! You're driving me crazy!"

"Fer Chrissakes!" Millard exclaimed and he left the living room and went to his study and shut the door. There was no winning from the first and he knew it. He was doomed from the start.

Dinner consisted of burnt grilled cheese sandwiches.

# Viagro 3

Monday morning at work Millard had a visitor. He sat outside the office. When Millard arrived, Jane appeared upset at having to deal with the man before the official starting time of nine. Millard knew Jane came early because she frequently expressed pleasure at giving herself time to ease into the day. As soon as Millard arrived, the man jumped to his feet. He was short and dark and had an intensity about him that was almost frightening.

"You Millard Fillmore?"

"Yes." Millard was disgruntled at the intrusion. He, too, liked to ease into the day. He also wanted to think about his problems with Ethel.

"I'd like to talk to you," the man said.

"You have an appointment?" Millard asked. He questioned Jane with a lift of the eyebrows. Millard wasn't formal but it seemed a good way to stall.

"No appointment," Jane said. She caught on quickly.

"Perhaps later, at a free moment, I can squeeze you in," Millard said. He smiled at Jane. Between them it was understood there wouldn't be any free moments.

But the man was not to be put off. He walked over to Millard and stepped in front of him and blocked the door.

"Look, Millard," he said, "I'm here on a personal matter of some importance."

"Personal?"

"Personal to you." He punctuated the word 'you' with a pointed index finger at Millard's chest.

Millard sighed and reached around the man and opened the door.

"Step in," he said.

The man strode into the office quickly. Millard placed his briefcase on the desk and walked around and sat down. The man sat and took out a notebook.

"I'm Nathan Guilder. I'm from The Enquirer."

"The what?"

"The National Enquirer."

"Look, ah, Mr. Guilder, we have a vice president in charge of public affairs. I'm sure he'll be able to answer any questions you might have."

"No," Nathan said, "I don't want to talk about the company. I want to talk about you."

"Me?"

"I understand you're the first man in recent modern history, at least that we know about, to maintain a perpetual erection."

"What? Where did you get that information?"

"And you have an agent by the name of Binky Derth."

"Oh?"

"And you're under medical and psychiatric care for that specific and unique problem."

"I have nothing to say," Millard said.

Nathan smiled. To Millard, he seemed to have an overdeveloped pair of canine teeth.

"You deny it?"

"I have no comment."

"You mind if I talk to your doctors?"

"Go ahead. They'll tell you nothing. Privileged communication and medical ethics and all that…"

"Ah-h-h, but they already have," Nathan said.

"Impossible."

"Not formally…but we have the files."

"Files?"

"Millard…c;'mon. We know the whole story. And from more than one source."

"Then what do you want from me? I have no comment. If you print, I'll sue."

Nathan Guilder pursed his lips. Millard decided he was a very ugly man.

"Tut, tut," Nathan said, "my paper prints nothing but the truth. We check and recheck. This is truth and we're going to print it. The world has a right to know. Besides, we have a lot of lawyers on retainer who need work."

"Get out," Millard said. "I'm calling my lawyer."

Nathan got up from his chair and snapped the notebook shut. He reached into his pocket and pulled out a card that he placed on the desk.

"OK," he said, "but if you change your mind and want to talk for the record, call me at this number."

Millard stared at Nathan and pointed to the door.

"Suit yourself," Nathan Guilder said and he left.

=We're going to be famous, Viagro exuded. He was all happy.

-Not if I can help it.

=What can you do? They probably caught the conversation at O'Neill's, checked out that Bruce waiter guy whom you nearly stiffed. I mean ten percent in this town is a stiff, really. And Binky, they probably got Binky drunk and he talked. And bribing medical secretaries is no problem.

-I'll sue!

=For what? Slander? Libel? Defamation? These guys are pros. I'll bet you they got copies of all the doctor reports. What about those files?

Are they safe? Haw! We're going to be famous, you and me. And I may get to see some action.

-Oh, lord.

=Don't oh lord me. This is it. This is the launching pad. It's champagne, caviar and wall-to-wall women!

Millard paced the office floor in high agitation. Jane came in and presented him with a cup of coffee. Millard took the cup and sat at his desk. Jane sat in front and spooned her drink.

"Who was he?" she asked.

"A reporter."

"Did you send him up to Hicks? He's in charge of PR now."

"Hicks? I thought Bonebar was."

"Not any more. Bonebar was transferred out and Hicks was transferred in."

"Lateral or demote?"

"Bonebar"s transfer was lateral but Hicks was down. What about the reporter?"

"Oh. He wanted to talk to me. It wasn't company business."

"What paper he from?"

"The National Enquirer."

Jane stopped playing with the coffee and looked up.

"The Enquirer?"

"Some story he thinks he's got."

"On you?"

Millard shrugged. "Yes."

"Whee! Who da thunk that? You embezzle anything? Are you keeping a child bride who's connected to aliens or what?"

"No. Don't be silly."

"Caught in a love nest with the world's ugliest woman?"

"No."

"Hobnobbing with stars in sleazy places?"

"No."

"Did you bite a dog?"

"No."

"I got it. You murdered your parents and shipped the bodies to New Zealand."

"No."

"Drugs then?"

"No."

"Male prostitution? You run male prostitutes?"

"No."

"Females? You sell girls?"

"No."

"What then? What would The Enquirer want with you?"

Millard leaned over the desk. He motioned for Jane to come closer. Jane leaned over and cocked her ear expectantly.

"You promise not to tell a soul?" Millard asked.

"I promise."

"Well, he was here to investigate The Claude Zimpfer File."

"The what?"

"The Claude Zimpfer File."

"Oh? Ha? Aha!" Jane giggled. "He's interested in that? C'mon. You're something, you are." Then her eyes went soft. "Hey, you in trouble?"

"Could be," Millard said.

Jane reached over and patted Millard's hand.

"I'm here if you need me," she said.

"I know. Thanks," Millard said.

Jane got up and walked over and got out the Zimpfer File. Her moves were, to Millard, deliberately provocative.

-What can I expect? Millard asked himself. After last Friday.

Jane placed the file on the desk as if she were delivering a treasure.

"Thought you might want to check it out," Jane said. She giggled and left Millard to ease into the day that was, at that point, clearly impossible.

Friday morning on the way to see Dr. Heatherton, Millard picked up a copy of The Enquirer. His picture was plastered on page one. "Super Stud?" was the caption, followed by "See story on page 3." The jump story was headlined. "Man's Dream Comes True; Super Virility Documented." It ran the full page. Millard groaned. The copy started with:

"Millard Fillmore, 40, of 678 Blitsmoan, Westchester, apparently is living out the all-time favorite male fantasy. According to medical documents in the possession of The Enquirer, Mr. Fillmore endures the enviable state of constant tumescence and will never have to worry about impotence or lack of vigor in performance ever again. Contacted earlier this week at his office by Enquirer Reporter Nathan Guilder where Mr. Fillmore is in charge of investments for Monmouth Insurance, Mr. Fillmore told The Enquirer 'no comment' when asked about his sex life. But the sharp-eyed twinkle belied this tepid response. We could tell Mr. Fillmore was a happy man in every way as…"

Millard staggered. He sat on a bench.

-I'm ruined…ruined.

=We're on our way, Viagro countered.

Millard crumpled the paper in disgust. He wanted to trash it but he thought better of it and refolded the sheet to show Dr. Heatherton whom he now desperately wanted to see.

When Dr. Heatherton read the article, she gasped.

"This is terrible," she said.

"I'm ruined," Millard said.

Dr. Heatherton wagged her head.

"I'm a little put out about this medical document reference," she said. "If there's a breech of security here, I'm going to find it." She glowered menacingly. Millard felt secure the culprit, if any, was in grave danger. "Now then," Dr. Heatherton said. "you must tell me how you feel about all this?"

"I'm ruined," Millard repeated.

"But how do you feel about it, down in your gut?"

"Doctor," Millard began, you know last week when I said I thought Viagro was growing?"

"Yes."

"Well, he talks now."

"What?"

"He talks."

"Ah, what does he say?"

"He made me proposition my own secretary."

"Made you?"

"Made is a little strong. He urged. He urged and then I did it. Well, not really but kind of."

Millard tried to read Dr. Heatherton's response. There was none to read.

"And did she respond?"

"Yes."

"And?"

"And we kind of postponed any action. I was surprised at her reaction."

"Oh."

"Viagro has a gravelly voice and he's obscene…"

"Obscene?"

"Yes, he wants me to do all kinds of crazy things like lay my secretary on the desk in some pornographic encounter. He's a troublemaker, no question."

"I see. He is, as I understand it, also a penis?"

"Yes."

"Well, isn't obscenity in the nature of a penis?"

"Uh, yes?"

"And if a penis could talk, would not that be his primary interest?"

"I suppose."

"So what exactly is the complaint?"

"He talks, dammit, and another thing. Ethel knows."

"Ethel? Your wife?"

"She knows."

"Knows what?"

"Of my hard-on problem. Has for weeks. So I told her I was seeing a doctor. But she got upset and we had a fight. It was over nothing, really. But things are still cool around the house. I'm not comfortable there."

"I see."

"And now this. This newspaper story is going to bitch things up at home and at work…and just about everywhere else."

"I see."

"Can't you say anything but 'I see'?"

"Yes…but we've got a lot of things happening here all at once. I'm trying to keep it straight."

=Tell the lady I'm straight…straight as it gets, Viagro said. With the exception of that slight little torque to the left.

-Shut up!

"Viagro just talked," Millard said.

"And what did he say?" Dr. Heatherton asked.

"He said, 'Tell the lady I'm straight'."

"Meaning?"

"Meaning he likes to interject shocking little things."

"Interject?"

"He pokes in, is that what you want me to say?"

"Not particularly. Poke isn't good here. And what did you say back…anything?"

"Oh, yes, I talk back."

"And?"

"I told him to shut up."

"And did he?"

"No, he thinks you're sexy and he wants an introduction."

"You tell him I said 'Hey' right back at him but we're all pretty busy right now," Dr. Heatherton said.

=Ask her if she's going to measure.

"Viagro wants to know if you're going to measure."

"Does he want measured?"

=You betcha!

"You betcha," he says.

"And what do you say?"

"Look, that's between you and him. Leave me out of it."

"Really?"

"Really."

Dr. Heatherton paused.

"Before we proceed any more along these lines, Millard, would you say Viagro is a separate being?"

"Yes."

"And he's growing stronger and more controlling?"

"Yes."

"And your worry is not now that he's growing physically, like last week, but he is now growing as an individual which threatens to take over your personality and life completely?"

Millard sighed. "That's it precisely."

"So we don't need to measure then, not physically."

=Shit!

"Viagro says: 'shit'.."

"Well, he would, wouldn't he? He's a penis. Naturally, he's disappointed. Penises are like that."

=Damn straight.

"Damn straight."

"Are you talking now for Viagro or yourself?"

"Viagro."

Millard motioned for Dr. Heatherton to lean close. She did and Millard whispered. "That's his whole act. He wants attention. He wants action. He's mad about it."

Dr. Heatherton nodded conspiratorially and leaned back.

"Why did you name him Viagro?" she asked. Her voice was one little decibel louder.

"Dunno. He was aggravating so I called him Aggro after the English contraction of aggravation. And somehow I just added a V and dropped a G. He really looks like Cyclops which was a one-eyed monster in mythology so I added an I, but Viagro seemed better."

"I see. I have read mythology. Now isn't that all rather literary for a business major?"

"I guess."

"Then where did you pick it up such esoteric information?"

"I don't know. High school Latin, maybe."

=I want laid!

"Oh, dear," Millard said.

"What?"

"Viagro is getting foul."

"What did he say?"

"I don't want to repeat it."

"What?"

"He said. 'I want laid'."

"I see. But then he is a penis and you are not. And you? Do you want laid?"

"I don't like your saying 'I see' all the time. It's irritating. And yes I do want laid. But his question is between him and you."

Dr. Heatherton shrugged.

"What do you want, Millard? What do you really want?"

"Out of this."

"Out of what?"

"This problem."

"Which problem?"

"All of them."

Millard flushed in anger and sat back in his chair. He felt tired, worn and defeated. Dr. Heatherton waited.

"Millard," she said at length. "I think it might be wise for you to be hospitalized."

"What?"

"Hospitalized."

Millard cupped his face in his hands. "Locked up?" He groaned.

"Hospitalized."

"No."

"I recommend it."

"It's not going to happen."

"Look, Millard, your inner and outer lives are in disarray. You're on the cover of The National Enquirer and I don't think just now you have the resources to cope."

=Tell her bullshit!

"Viagro says, 'bullshit'."

"What do you say?"

"I say 'bullshit,' too."

"I see."

Millard raised his hand. He'd heard enough 'I see'.

"How about all right?" Dr. Heatherton quickly offered.

"OK," Millard said. "But no hospital. I understand you can force hospital only on those who are a danger to themselves or others?

"All right."

"Well, nobody I ever heard of got clubbed to death with a penis. So that's it then. I'll call if I need to talk. But I'd rather stay out of the locked wards and do this on my own."

=Good boy!

-Right!

"Right," Millard said aloud to Dr. Heatherton.

"Right?" Dr. Heatherton asked.

"I see," said Millard and he left.

Millard bolted from Dr. Heatherton's office, caught the elevator and rushed to a phone. Once there, he looked up Binky Derth's company and dialed its switchboard.

"Binky Derth in sales," Millard said.

Millard heard a sigh.

"Is this in reference to company business?" the operator asked.

"Of course," said Millard. He puzzled over the question and then it hit him. Binky was named as his agent in the article. His phone must be ringing off the hook. Millard had a sinking feeling his own phones would also be ringing, both at work and at home.

"Binky Derth's office."

"Millard Fillmore for Binky Derth."

"Millard Fillmore? The Millard Fillmore? The man who…?"

"The same."

"Oh, wow! One moment, please."

There were some clicks.

"Millard? Millard? Jesus Christ, where are you? Things are crazy here. Crazy."

"Binky, you want to be my agent?"

"Sure I do. I'm already named. I'll sue if I'm not."

"I'm not going to ask about how the story broke or how the press got the information, OK?"

"OK."

"And you can be my agent."

"Wow! Millard?"

"Yes?"

"Is it true?"

"Is what true?"

"What the medical reports say. Do you have the, ah, condition?"

"It's true."

"Then we're on. Twenty percent OK?"

"Ten's better."

"Fifteen?"

"Fifteen. Draw up the contract."

"Done. Listen, Millard, things are going to get hairy from here on out. Let me give you my answering service number. It's STI-FY69, now, ain't that cute? I want you to call at least three times a day."

Millard took out a pen, tore off part of a page of the telephone book and jotted down the number and seriously wondered if he had entrusted his life into quite the right hands.

"Got it," Millard said.

"And stay available," Binky said.

"No problem," Millard said. "I'm nothing if not available."

"Good," Binky said. "Millard, I'm going to make you a star."

"Yeah," Millard said. He hung up. He tried to call his office but the line was busy. So was the line to home. Millard left the phone booth and hiked to the subway. He thought he detected a few stares but there was no incident, no catcalls or obscene signs. Once at Forty Second Street, Millard disembarked. He scrunched his face down in his shirt so it would be less obvious and walked to his office. The office was in disarray and Jane looked frazzled. She glanced at his face and then dropped her eyes and stared at his crotch.

"They've heard?" Millard asked.

"Right," Jane said. "The president want to see you at once."

Jane's eyes never left Millard's crotch.

"Is it true?" she asked.

"It's true," Millard said.

Jane's eyebrows furrowed, then she smiled, then she frowned.

"I don't know what to say," she admitted.

"Me neither," Millard said.

He turned and walked out. As he passed each office, girls dropped things and ran to the door to stare. Men Millard had known for years gawked. It was as if Millard never existed and some apparition was walking in his place, an apparition that generated surprise and awe. Millard caught the elevator to the executive suite. Once there, he approached the president's secretary. She reacted like Jane and riveted her eyes on his zipper. "Go right in," she said.

President Myron Blower sat at his desk. A copy of the paper was on his desk. In fact, it was the only thing on his desk. Myron's face was tinted red and the color really set off his mane of white hair. He glared as Millard walked in and sat down.

"I've been reading about you," he said. "Christ, the whole world's been reading about you."

Millard shrugged.

"Is that all you've got to say?" Myron snapped.

Millard shrugged again. "I haven't said anything."

"Tell me about it," Myron commanded.

"Some weeks ago I got an erection and it never left. My doctor gave me some experimental pills because ah, you know. And then I got worried and went back to my doctor. He sent me to a psychiatrist. That's it."

"And you've still got the…ah…problem?"

"Yes."

"Still seeing the shrink?"

"Yes." Millard mentally added now and then to his statement.

"Then what about this article?" Myron waved the paper under Millard's nose.

"A couple of days ago Nathan Guilder appeared in my office. I gave him no comment. It's in the article. Says right there, 'no comment'."

"Christ, don't you know a journalist can write a hundred words on yes, five hundred words on no," and a thousand on no comment!"

"I do now."

"Damn," Myron fumed, "this is bad for us…bad exposure for the company. Monmouth Insurance, home of Millard Fillmore."

Millard winced.

"I know. I'm sorry. It's not so pleasant for me personally, either."

"I imagine not," Myron said. "I think what would be best for both of us would be for you to run out your sick time and then take an extended vacation on administrative leave with pay and, after that, if this isn't all cleared up, a permanent leave of absence."

"Right."

"That way the company name won't be dragged into it any further."

"My thoughts exactly," Millard said.

"I've always liked you, Millard," Myron said. "You were the quickest prime interest rate quoter guy in the history of this company." Myron's eyes teared and he sniffled.

"Thank you, sir. I knew my primes."

"Well, get cracking. Write me from time to time."

"I shall. And, Myron?"

"Yes?"

"Those investments you recommended last month?"

"Uh huh?"

"They bombed. Went to hell. Shit canned a bushel of cash. Zipped. Tubed. It was a total fart out."

Myron's face fell. "Damn," he muttered.

Millard's voice picked up with new enthusiasm. "But I recommend, sir, you say I recommended them," Millard offered.

"I can't," Myron sputtered. "I made that recommendation at a board meeting."

"Oh, yes," Millard said. "I remember." Myron twisted up the corners of the National Enquirer and grimaced. "While you're at it," Millard continued, "at the board I mean, you'll have to tell them its investment recommendations also bombed."

"Theirs too?"

"Yes." Millard was enjoying himself.

"What's total loss?" Myron asked.

"I figure a loss of revenue of some six and a half million dollars this quarter alone."

"Six. Six!? Six and a half million dollars?"

"Right…give or take a few thousand either way." Millard arose. "I'll write," he said and he walked out of the office. Myron worked his eyebrows up and down and his face went from scarlet to crimson and he sucked air like he was on oxygen.

Millard went directly to his office and ignored stares from his fellow workers. In fact, he grew defiant in a way and pushed his hips forward as he walked. Jane's sheaf of phone messages filled her 'out' basket. She was on the phone when Millard arrived and the console pulsed with the flashing lights of incoming calls. Jane looked up at Millard and in her face was a blend of hurt and anger.

"Jane?" Millard called. Jane put a hand over the receiver and waited. "Just let the phones ring. No more messages. I need to talk to my wife so try and get her, will you? And then I'll need you in my office."

Jane nodded. She purred, "I'll see he gets the message" into the phone and hung up.

Once in the office, Millard cleaned out his desk. He was sure the vacation and leave of absence suggestion was ploy to move him out. He'd seen it before. Insurance companies were more restrained but just as ruthless as politics or government. Millard had time to pack his things and tidy up before Jane got a line to Ethel. When his intercom buzzed, Millard already was bored and restless. He tapped into the intercom.

"I have a line ringing into your home," Jane announced.

"Good," Millard said, "how'd you do it?"

"I told the operator it's an emergency."

"Well, it is," Millard said and he switched to his phone and waited as the ringing continued.

"Hello!" Ethel shouted.

"Ow," Millard exclaimed as he pulled the receiver from his ear. "Hey, honey, take it easy. It's me."

"Oh, it is, is it? Well, thanks to you, the phone's been ringing off the hook with everything from horny ladies to fast-buck artists."

"I'm sorry."

"Sorry doesn't cut it here. My friends keep coming in and leaving a copy of that damn paper. Millard, this is terrible! Do you know what you've done to us, to the kids, to everybody?"

"What can I say?"

"Yes, what can you say?"

"I lost my job for one. Oh, it's not official. Myron asked me to run out sick time and then take an administrative leave until the smoke clears. But I think they're easing me out. I'm pretty sure it's all over."

"Won-der-full!" Jane hesitated. "Millard, I don't know how to put this…but I'd rather you didn't come home for a while. I need some time here and so do the kids. Can you imagine what it must be like for them at school?" She cried. "Oh, Millard, how could you?"

"I didn't ask for all this," Millard said. "I just took a damn blue pill."

"OK, OK, I know. Listen, can you give me a few days? I might be able to talk rationally by then…"

"Sure," Millard said. He hung up. Instead of feeling sad, Millard was surprised to find he felt relieved. His job and wife were almost gone and instead of fear there was expectation; instead of panic there was peace, and instead of loss he felt oddly filled.

=Well, I did it, Viagro announced.
-You did it?
=Sure, Viagro said. You'd have never done it. I've freed you up.
-Why?
=I'm tired of lackluster.
-Me, too. But this?
=Sure, this. What else? We're going where the action is.
-We are?
=You'll see. Binky's working his little buns off. You'll see.

"Millard?" Jane called. She stood in front of him.

"Oh, yes?" Millard replied.

Jane sat down.

"I see you're packing."

"Yes, Myron told me to run out sick leave. Then, if things aren't settled, to take an administrative leave."

"What's to become of me?"

"Oh," Millard said, "you'll be OK. You're a crack secretary and they can't run this office without you. If I don't come back, you'll get a new boss to train."

Jane looked down at her lap.

"Millard, I've been with you a long time," she said quietly.

"I know."

"I'll miss you."

"I'll miss you."

Millard and Jane fell silent.

"How's Ethel taking it?" Jane asked.

"Bad. She wants me to leave for a few days. I've been kicked out. She's mad and not a little grossed."

Jane's eyes narrowed.

"You going to leave her?" she asked.

"Maybe. And maybe she'll leave me."

Jane sighed.

"Where you going to stay?"

"I'll be checking into the West Side 'Y' until I get it together."

"You could stay with me," Jane said. "Not every body is grossed out."

Millard looked at her closely. He could tell she'd given the matter some thought. There was no hesitation in voice or manner.

"I'd like to," Millard admitted. "But things are so crazy right now I'd like to hide."

"I understand," Jane said. "You've got my address and phone number. I want you to know I'll be taking home a copy of the Claude Zimpfer File and it'll be at my place permanently for your on call inspection."

Millard smiled and reached over and patted Jane's hand.

"Thanks," he said.

=This is Number One, Viagro said. Take her up on the offer!

"Thanks for your kindness," Millard said. He ignored Viagro.

Jane's eyes shined and she smiled weakly.

"A prime rump should not be wasted," she said.

"Oh?"

"It's OK," she said. She got up and left the room. Millard heard her sniffle. Millard sighed, picked up his things and left.

=Free at last, free at last, free at last! Viagro chanted as Millard stepped onto the streets of Manhattan and headed for the subway.

Millard's room at the 'Y' was on the seventh floor. He had a northern exposure. Millard unlocked his closet and dumped his office things inside. Then he dug through them to find a pencil and paper. He sat on the bed and listed things he'd have to buy. The list grew quickly as items such as toothpaste and razors and underpants sparked a whole sequence of needs. Discouraged by the length of the list, Millard tossed the pencil aside and went down to the lobby to call Binky. He gave the answering service his name, location and room number. Millard then went back to his room to work on his list. Just when he'd warmed to the task, his buzzer sounded. Millard stood up and stared at the instrument. He quickly scanned the explanation sheet posed near it. The sequenced blaring into his ears signaled a phone call. Millard buzzed back, as the card told him, and went in search of a hall phone. Once he located the hall phone, he followed posted directions. He called the desk and told them his name, room number and phone extension number. Then he was told to hang up and wait for the phone to ring. He did so. When it rang and he picked it up, Binky was on the line.

"Mill? Jesus! I'm glad you called!" Binky was breathless and excited.

"I'm at the 'Y'," Millard said.

"I know. I dialed. Listen, can you meet us at O'Neill's in twenty minutes?"

"Us? Just who is us?"

"Never you mind. Us is good people. You'll see!"

"Binky, what have you done?"

"You'll find out. I'm talking product line here. I'm talking book!"

"What?"

"Be there!" Binky said. The phone clicked in Millard's ear.

Millard hung down the receiver slowly. Binky's enthusiasm scared him but it also made him curious. Millard found himself strangely elated. He turned around and faced a young man clad only in a towel. The young man was blonde and wore his hair long. The tresses were wavy and sleek. He had apparently been staring at Millard during the phone call. He'd been staring at a certain place.

"Excuse me," the young man said, "but aren't you Millard Fillmore?"

"Yes," Millard said.

The boy lifted his left hand to his forehead and tilted his head back in a gesture of great shock.

"The Millard Fillmore?"

"Yes."

The boy sighed and rolled his eyes up into his head.

"Oh!" he exclaimed, "I feel I'm in the presence of a god!"

Millard grew immediately frightened so he smiled and rushed past the young man who staggered and flailed air with his arms.

"A god. A god. It's enough to give a girl the vapors," the boy called as Millard made good his escape by ducking around a corner.

# Viagro 4

O'Neill's Balloon was moderately busy and Millard checked out the mural as he stepped into the door. The painting never ceased to please him. He looked around. Binky was in the northeast corner table that was up on a platform. He sat with two men and the table was piled high with attache cases and papers. Binky's tie was askew and he wore little half glasses that made him look owlish. Millard brushed by the maitre'd and walked to the table. As soon as Binky saw him, Binky waved. By the time Millard arrived at the table, Binky stood, peered over his glasses and fumbled the paper that he held in his hands. The two men sat silently.

"Hi," Binky said. "Sit down."

Millard sat.

"This is Myron Gluts and this is Ben Gross," said Binky. He waved in the general direction of the men.

"Hello," Millard said. Myron and Ben nodded. Both smoked cigars. As they nodded, both shifted their cigars from one side of their mouth to the other.

"OK," Binky said, "you and I got some preliminary business."

"Oh?" Millard asked.

"I been busy," Binky said. He looked proud. He rustled around in the pile of papers and came up with a packet. "This is our contract, the agent's agreement. It's simple, short and to the point." Millard scanned the document. He saw the percentage point he was looking for and um-hummed approval. It was right. "Sign it," Binky said.

"Don't I get to read it?" Millard asked.

"Sure," Binky said," but time is precious. This whole deal depends on time. You have what options market players call a 'wasting asset'."

Millard burst out laughing. "I've never heard of a hard-on described that way, but now I think about it, it seems right. Real right." Millard continued to laugh until the tears started out the corners of his eyes. Then he gasped, cleared his throat, shook his head and composed himself. Myron and Ben looked on unmoved. Binky waited.

"Sign," Binky said.

"Can I trust you?" Millard asked.

"You have to trust me some time, why not now?" Binky countered.

"OK." Millard said. He signed. Myron and Ben glanced at each other and smiled. Binky pulled out another sheaf of papers that he shoved under Millard's nose.

"These are articles of incorporation. Our lawyers…"

"Lawyers?" Millard cut in.

"Lawyers. I hired us a firm, a good one."

"Oh."

"They think maximum profit from a venture like this will come from a corporation rather than, say, a partnership. Less risk. Greater tax advantages in the long run."

Millard lifted the packet and weighed it. "This is pretty hefty," he said.

"Trust me," Binky said. Millard sighed. He felt elated. His instincts kept crying out for restraint but his new self felt confident and dashing. He liked the feeling of living on the edge so he signed with authority and ended his signature with a flourish. Binky smiled. "Good," he said. Binky placed the articles in an attache case and then laid the agent's agreement on top. He handled the documents carefully.

"I'll need copies," Millard said. He couldn't help it. His conservative nature just broke through.

"Sure," Binky said, "no problem." He reached in his pocket and took out three credit cards. He placed them in front of Millard. All had his name on them. They said 'Millard Fillmore, Inc'. "What do you think?" Binky asked. He beamed.

"Great," Millard said.

"Right," Binky said. "I move fast." Binky leaned over the table. "Use these cards for everything, even toothpaste. Thanks to Myron and Ben here, we got no money problems. Every card is open-end. "He sat back and smiled. Then he turned to Myron. "OK, Myron, you're on."

"Right," Myron rasped. He took the cigar from his mouth "I run a sex aid company. We carry everything from pills to paraphernalia. I got in mind for you for starters a potency pill, 'The Millard Fillmore Potency Capsule'. We'll have your picture on the label and in the ads…"

"Ads?"

"Ads," Myron continued. "We're starting this week with full pages in The Enquirer and all like that. And later this month, in the men's mags like Playboy and all that. We got us in mind a class act here. No sleaze. We've all agreed to no sleaze. I've got us a red, bullet-shaped spansule with a bull head logo. The logo's right, the shape's right, the color's right…"

"And all you need is my picture?" Millard asked.

"And the name," Myron added.

"Our cut's nice," Binky said.

"We split the net fifty-fifty," Myron said.

Millard turned to Binky. Binky smiled and nodded.

"Myron and Ben are worth it, Millard. They're putting up front money for now and buying the ads and stuff, printing labels, tying us into a mail operation, advancing expenses."

"What expenses?" Millard asked."I'm living at the 'Y.' I've got one suit."

"Yeah, right,"Binky said, "and you're moving from there right now."

"I am?"

"You are. I'm taking you and your cards to a suite in the St. Moritz. We want you there. It's a classy place but not uppity like The Plaza or flash-modern like, say, The Americana. It's got the right image for us: it's respectable. From there we'll hike on down to Brooks Brothers where they're putting you together with your new wardrobe. I want the Brooks look, understated and rich. Preppy, you know? I already contacted them and they're waiting.

"You're kidding," Millard said.

"I'm serious," Binky said.

"I'm serious," Myron said. "I'm committing a half mil."

"Million?" Millard asked.

"Dollars," Myron said.

Millard stared down at the table. He felt in shock.

"Millard, Millard," Binky purred as he patted Millard's arm, "you're a marketable commodity, an eminently marketable commodity." Millard was confused. He wanted to change the subject.

"What's in the pills?" Millard asked Myron. He spit out the question abruptly and Myron jumped at the quick shift.

"Vitamin E. We may put in some caffeine," he said, warming to the subject, "but nothing unproven or harmful. Vitamin E has some benefit and all the research for it as a sex performance enhancer can be ours if we have to go to court to support our ad claims. Actually, the pill's already on the market. We're just repackaging under your name. No sweat."

"Oh," Millard said.

"After Brooks," Binky said, "we go to the photographer. He's got his own hairdresser. The Brooks salesman knows exactly which suit we've picked for the session and he's doing the preliminary work now."

"Fast, it's going awfully fast here," Millard murmured.

"Sure," Binky said. He turned and looked at Ben. "You're on." Ben leaned forward and took the cigar out of his mouth. Myron leaned back and placed the cigar further back in his mouth.

"OK," Ben said, "I'm getting a book out with your picture on it and your sex advice in it. I figure it'll be out in ten days. It's like 'Joy of Sex' because we use drawings that are detailed but tasteful. The copy, however, is more appealing and your knowledge and experience shows."

"It does?" Millard asked. "Fancy that." He thought his knowledge and experience might be puffed up to one whole typewritten page, if expanded. But a whole book was out of the question.

"Right," Ben said, "you talk like the authority you are. This book's a sure winner."

"In ten days?" Millard asked. "And I'm an authority?"

"Well," Ben said, "the book is already written and we have the rights. We're just plugging you into the copy because we figure you're the vehicle to move it. All we need is your face and name."

"That's it?" Millard asked.

"That's it. And we split these profits fifty-fifty after expenses, same as Myron."

Millard sat back and sighed. He was stunned. Binky nudged him.

"You like these ideas?" Binky asked.

"I don't know. I think so," Millard said.

"Good," Binky said. He shoved two more contracts at him. "Sign here." Millard went numb. He signed the documents slowly. Myron and Ben picked up the contracts as soon as they were signed and tucked them away in cases.

"Good to do business with you," Myron said.

"Likewise," Ben said.

Both men arose and left. Binky shoved all the papers into his case and looked at Millard.

"It's going to be OK," he said, "more than OK. Hell, it's going to be great." He looked at his watch. "Let's get rolling, we've got work to do." He grabbed Millard by the arm and rushed him out of O'Neill's. Millard stumbled to keep up. Once outside of O'Neill's, Binky hailed a cab.

"Brooks Brothers," he commanded the driver as he stuffed Millard into the back seat. The cab took off down Broadway.

"OK, Millard," Binky said, "you got to understand the PR tack we're taking. Our consultants…"

"Consultants?"

"I hired us a PR firm. It's one of the best. Our consultants agree with me we'll get farther faster if we present a sense of dignity here…"

"A dignified hard-on? You're presenting a dignified erection?"

"Precisely. We got to package your condition with class. Otherwise, we got sleaze."

"So I dress Brooks and stay at the St. Moritz."

"Exactly. What we're putting together here is the making of authority, not because of study or training but because of experience and a generous gift from nature."

"Look," Millard said, "I took a damn blue pill. It was experimental. It screwed up. That ain't nature."

Binky shrugged.

"And for an authority, I haven't even gotten laid yet. And my premarital experiences you could jot on a fingernail."

"Doesn't matter. The condition matters. The image matters. The perception matters. We present you as you are, a decent guy with a hard-on."

"Is there such a person?"

"There is now. A decent man with a hard-on who wants to share his experience, give good advice and bring dignity and class to sex itself."

Millard sat back in the cab seat and drew up into himself. "Like that's going to happen."

"It's the Steve Martin ploy," Binky said. "Steve didn't hit it big until he dressed like an insurance salesman. We got the same thing here. If we dress you like a show stud then all we got is a show stud, a John Holmes clone. But if we dress you conservative and capitalize on your nice guy image, we got a class act to sell to middle America."

"Christ," Millard exploded, "do people get paid to think this way?"

"Sure. Every day. It's where the big bucks are."

"Brooks," the driver growled.

"Good," Binky said. He threw the driver a ten. "Keep the change."

"Thanks," the cabbie said. He turned around, looked at Binky, and then at Millard. "Hey," he said, "ain't you Millard Fillmore?"

"Yes," Millard said.

The cabbie fumbled in the front seat and shoved a greasy piece of paper under the plastic shield.

"I been readin' about you. Can I have your autograph? It's for the wife."

Millard looked at Binky. Binky smiled and nodded.

"Sure," Millard said. "What's your wife's name?"

"Conchita."

Millard signed the paper: "To Conchita, with undying respect, and for all those good times. Love, Millard Fillmore." He handed the paper to the cabbie. He read it and looked back.

"Gee, thanks, Mr. Fillmore," he said. "She's gonna love this."

Binky grinned and heaved a sigh. "We're golden," he whispered to Millard, "absolutely golden."

"Bink, do you realize I could have signed it: 'Thanks for one toe curling blow job and all the super screwings we shared'," Millard said "and the cabbie would have still loved it?"

"I know," Binky said, "I know." And he just kept repeating the word "golden."

Brooks Brothers smelled good to Millard. There was a scent in fine wools that always pleased and Brooks had it in abundance. The store wasn't crowded; there were a few refugees from The Athletic Club fingering patch pants but that was all. When Millard and Binky arrived, two men rushed forward. One had his jacket off and a tape measure hung around his neck. The other was fully dressed, complete with vest. They smiled.

"Help you?" the fully-dressed man asked. The man with the tape measure grinned.

"Yes," Binky said, "this is Millard Fillmore. I called ahead? I'm Binky Derth."

"Of course," said the salesman. "We've been expecting you." The tailor with the tape measure bowed slightly and scurried to the back of the store. "Come with me," said the salesman.

He led Binky and Millard deeper and deeper into the store until they were at a final bank of suits. A triple mirror was set in the middle. The tailor appeared from behind with a black, pin-stripe suit. He placed the pants on a case and opened the jacket and helped Millard try it on. When Millard's arms were through the sleeves, the tailor brushed the suit coat's shoulders flat and stepped around and buttoned the front. Then he tugged lightly at the front and stepped back to look.

"Perfect," he said. "We'll have no trouble here, Mr. Derth, that's a forty two regular."

"How's it feel?" Binky asked Millard. Millard moved his shoulders and the jacket adapted easily to his movements.

"Fits like a glove," Millard said. He'd never worn a jacket quite so comfortable. "Except," he added, "isn't the color and style too severe?"

"No," Binky said, "it's just right."

"But it's a suit for an investment banker," Millard said. "I'm not an investment banker."

"You may be one soon," Binky noted.

"No,"Millard said, "it's too severe. This suit should be worn by a diplomat or something."

Binky walked up to Millard and pulled him aside.

"This is image, Millard, the image we want to project. In a way, you are a diplomat, a diplomat representing a really touchy subject. Your whole wardrobe is like this, shoes, ties, shirts, everything."

"This isn't me," Millard protested, "I'm Bloomingdale at best and then only when they have a sale."

"It's you now," Binky snapped. "I've ordered ten outfits here from top to bottom and every one has been approved by our PR people."

"Socks? What about socks? You got socks?" Millard asked. His tone was defiant.

"Socks we also got," Binky answered.

"Shoes?"

"Shoes."

"Belts?"

"Belts."

"Undershorts?"

"Undershorts."

"PJ's. What about PJ's?"

"PJ's."

"Ah, toiletries?"

"No."

"Aha! I need a toothbrush, some toothpaste and an electric razor and a comb and some shaving lotion."

Binky smiled. "We'll get them," he said. Millard turned aside. He felt exhausted. Binky walked over to the salesman. He talked and the salesman took out a notepad and wrote. The tailor asked Millard to try on the suit pants. Millard jockeyed Viagro around and tried them on. The tailor measured the length of the pants; then he measured Millard from top to bottom: neck, chest, arms, waist, hips, wrist, feet.. everything. Millard felt like a side of prize beef.

"OK," Binky called, "grab the jacket, they'll deliver the rest." Millard sighed. "And a shirt and tie," Binky added. "We'll need the shirt and tie with it."

"Why?" Millard asked.

"Because all the photographer is going to shoot is your head and shoulders. We call it a headshot," Binky said.

"Figures," Millard said. He smiled to himself. Headshot? Such irony was beyond Binky.

The tailor stepped forward and looked into Millard's eyes.

"I want you to know, Mr. Fillmore," he said quietly, "you bring hope to all us tired old men."

"You're not old," Millard blurted.

"No, but I am tired," the tailor said. He smiled. "Your inspiring story has brought hope to us all." He turned and walked away.

-Millard thought the man had probably taken one too many inside leg measurement.

"C'mon," Binky called, "we're late already."

Millard followed. He thought about what the tailor said.

-Perhaps, he told himself, there are some redeeming social values in all of this.

The photographer's studio was in the upper east seventies. The operation had taken over two floors of a medium-sized building. Binky shoved Millard into the beauty salon.

"Hey? You got an order on Millard Fillmore here?" Binky called.

"Sure thing," said the young man who stepped forward. He was lithe, tanned and handsome. He wore a cape of singularly incandescent color and design. A head strap of the same material held back long hair. He looked like a day-glo Roman. "We certainly do," he said. He held out his hand. Binky shook it quickly.

"I'm Bruce," said the young man.

"Of course you are. And you got our order?" Binky pressed.

"Not to worry," said Bruce.

"Is your name really Bruce?" Millard asked.

"No," Bruce said, "it's Rocky Cluzowski from Cleveland but I changed it because I wanted to be a stereotype." He pirouetted and bowed. With the flowing cape billowing, it was really dramatic.

"Wonderful," Binky said, "We love to hear life stories. OK, Bruce, fix my man up here. I'll be back in a little bit."

"Fine," Bruce said. He turned to Millard. "What a fucking Philistine. Right this way, darling."

"Darling? Don't darling me, Bruce, or I will call you Rocky."

Bruce's face fell.

"Oh, but you are a darling," Bruce said, "and I'm going to make you America's darling."

"Fine," Millard said, "but I'm not your darling."

"OK," Bruce smirked. "But with your equipment you're bound to be somebody's darling, trust me."

"You can be Rocky but I can't be your darling, you got that Bruce?"

"Sure. But you're the one with the Rock that makes you darling."

"OK, Rock, you be Bruce, but I've got the rock and I'm not a Bruce, so I can't be your darling, do you understand? I'm Millard."

Bruce sighed, looked nostalgic and then a little sad. "Can we stop having this conversation?"

"Of course," Millard said, "if you remain clear on your Bruces and rocks and darlings."

"I think I have it," Bruce said solemnly, "And I'm sure there was something in that conversation somewhere."

"I'm sure there was," Millard cut in. "Only neither of us found it."

"But whatever it was I now have it," Bruce said and he smiled.

"Good," Millard said. "You Bruce, me Millard."

"Fine," Bruce said, "come along."

"OK," Millard said. But he winced.

Bruce led Millard far into the salon. In the back were chairs, sinks and dryers. Bruce helped Millard into the chair.

"First we shampoo," Bruce said, "then we cut and style; then we shampoo again and then we fluff, blow dry and comb and set."

"Oh," Millard said. He didn't know exactly what all that meant but he got an idea as the chair in which he was sitting suddenly went horizontal and Bruce threw a sheet over him. Millard settled in and found his head was neatly near a water basin and Bruce got busy with hoses.

"After I'm done," Bruce said, "the make up people take over."

"Make up?"

"Oh, yes, they're very important for a session like this."

Millard sighed and closed his eyes. The procedure seemed to take forever even though Bruce worked quickly. When the make up people came, they were also swift but still Millard had a sense of drag time. Millard missed the chatter he'd always experienced in a barber's chair but he also realized his non-conversation with Bruce precluded any more verbal interchange. Besides, he didn't want to hear Bruce's chatter. And the make up people were all business so conversation was out of the question.

"OK, darling, we're done," Bruce announced at last.

"I told you I'm not your darling," Millard countered. "We've been through that."

"Oops, sorry," Bruce said. "Force of habit. Shall I call you Rock?"

"Millard! Call me Millard."

"Of course."

Millard sat up and looked in the mirror. Now Bruce was getting snippy. He was amazed that now his face fit the suit. The gray in his hair was highlighted; Bruce had fluffed it out over his ears. The top of his hair sported a really distinguished gray streak that was tastefully combed back and blended. The entire contour of his hair had changed and his hair looked fuller and more weighted. The shadows of his face were softened and selected highlights were accentuated. His eyebrows had somehow been enhanced, as had his eyes and eyelids and lashes. He looked older and more distinguished than he thought ever possible. In fact, he concluded, he looked like a model in a Scotch Liquor ad. Bruce looked on and admired his own work.

"Breathtaking, isn't it?" Bruce asked.

"Yeah," Millard said, "I got to admit it is."

He had to agree. There was no other word for it. Binky walked into the room. He stopped and stared.

"Holy shit," Binky said. Bruce beamed. Millard shrugged. "This is going better than I'd hoped," Binky said. Binky walked into an outer room and returned with the suit coat, the shirt and the tie. He handed the clothes to Millard. "Put these on," he said. "We're late as is but it's OK because the photographer is running late." Millard stood up and Bruce unwrapped him. Then Millard put on the shirt. "Don't wrinkle it," Binky said. He paused. "Maybe it'd be better if you didn't tuck it in or tie the tie," Binky said, "they got people to do that for you." Millard stood with shirt and tie askew and held the suitcoat on a hanger. "C'mon," Binky said, "that's close enough." Binky led Millard quickly out of the salon.

"Toodle oo," Bruce called.

"Thanks, Rock," Millard called back.

-Straight people can get snippy too, you know.

"A pleasure, darling," Bruce responded.

-Damn, thought Millard. He got the last shot.

Millard and Binky caught an elevator to the top floor. They stepped out into what seemed pandemonium; people scurried about; some carried large lights; some carried scenic backdrops; some toted sawhorses and others chatted to one another and marked things on clipboards. At the center of the maelstrom stood a tall, lean man in a paisley beret and a matching scarf. Only he seemed calm.

-Well, thought Millard, he must be the eye of this hurricane. Or maybe he was the center of this mad vortex. It was one or the other and perhaps both.

Binky walked up to the man in the beret. Millard followed.

"Jacques, meet Millard. Millard, meet the finest photographer in New York or any other city, Jacques Breel."

"Jacques Breel? Isn't that, ah…?" Millard said.

"That's right," Jacques cut in, "I'm named after a literary allusion. Or perhaps a character. I can never keep it straight."

"That's odd," Millard said, "I just met a hairdresser who wanted to be a stereotype."

"Of course," Jacques said, "I only hire my kind of people around here. I also have a cameraman who thinks he's a consonant but then he isn't very imaginative."

"Wonderful," Binky said, "you word play dorks about ready for Millard?"

"And a scheduling assistant who thinks she's a vowel," Jacques continued, ignoring Binky. "But I'm not going to expand on that."

"OK," Binky said, "but are you ready for Millard?"

"I don't think the world is ready for Millard," Jacques said and he chortled. It was odd to see a man in a paisley beret chortle. Then he studied Millard carefully. "Um-hum.. um-hummm," he went. Millard waited. "Have you ever thought of yourself as a total adverb?"

"No," Millard replied.

"Not even a teensy weensy pronoun?"

"No," Millard said. But then he jumped into the spirit of things, "I've always thought of myself as a misplaced modifier."

"Marvelous!" Jacques said. "I couldn't do better." He turned to Binky. "I'll have him dressed and then we'll look for the shoot concept. That's very important you know." He turned and walked away.

"What was that all about?" Binky said.;

"I don't know," Millard said, "but joining up with lunacy is a lot easier than trying to understand it."

Binky shrugged. "He came highly recommended," Binky muttered.

Two assistants approached Millard. Very carefully they tucked in his shirt. Next, one tied and installed the tie while the other helped Millard with his coat. Millard felt lighthearted and frivolous.

"Are either of you parts of speech?" he asked.

"Hell, no," said one. "What kind of creeps you think we are?" The second assistant smiled.

"Oh," Millard said, "I'm sorry."

"No offense," the second assistant said, "Mike, here is new and hasn't adjusted to all this." Mike frowned. "I got no truck with this shit because I'm a teamster and I've chosen to be a fugue and Mike here's training to be a rondo."

"Whatever the hell that is," Mike growled.

"I thought as much," Millard said. He smiled and thought now we got music men. The second assistant smiled. Mike shrugged and twisted his mouth in undisguised irritability.

"This is a funny farm is what it is," Mike said, "but it pays top dollar. A man can put up with a lot for top dollar." The second assistant shrugged and walked away. Mike followed.

"I want to get the hell out of here," Binky whispered. "These people are weird. In fact, the whole place is weird."

"Relax," Millard said, "it's kind of fun. Go out there and be an iambic pentameter or something."

"What?"

"Never mind."

Jacques Breel returned. He looked at Millard coolly and professionally.

"I see you," he said, "but I don't really see you."

"Please?" Binky said.

"I see the man. I see the artistic problem. I visualize the condition. I know the assignment. But I haven't yet grasped the crucial interior concept, clutched hold of that overriding insight that pulls this shot together."

"Please?" Binky repeated. "We are shooting a damn advertisement here."

A naked woman walked up and stood beside Jacques. Her only nod to any attempt at clothes was a pair of black high-heel shoes. Her melon breasts thrust forward and her long blonde hair framed a strikingly beautiful face. Millard could see the nipples of her breasts were rouged and her whole body had been powdered. She stared defiantly at Jacques. Millard and Binky shifted uncomfortably and tried to avert their eyes.

"I think you're wrong, Jacques," she said. She pointed to her pubic hair. "The area you wish to minimize is also the main area of interest to my public." Jacques drew himself up and huffed.

"We're talking proportion here. We're talking eye-line. We're talking professional judgment," he snorted.

The blonde turned to Millard and Binky. "I ask you as impartial observers and men who are not observably gay," she said, "do you think my triangle here is too broad, too dominant, too blonde even? This beast wants to shave it down."

"Getting coiffed is part of posing," Jacques sniffed. "I do not highlight small furry animals. If you want to break into centerfolds, you must accept that."

"Ah, no," Binky stammered. He stared at the woman's shoes.

Millard paused. "I have to agree with Jacques," Millard said, "as your pudenda stands, the angles of the triangle are way too broad. I think the area needs diminished, not much, mind you, but just a tad. Otherwise, you'll wind up with a picture of one huge intransitive verb down there and then where will your public be…out searching for an adjective or something?"

Jacques clapped his hands. "Wonderful!" he exclaimed, "I couldn't have said it better myself."

Binky glared at Millard. Millard shrugged and held up his hands. The blonde huffed and walked away.

"I think I've solved our problem," Millard said to Jacques.

"Really?" Jacques asked.

Binky dropped his head and shook it.

"Yes," Millard continued, "the interior concept you need just came to me."

"Go on," Jacques said.

Millard walked up and put his hand on Jacques' shoulder. He stared off into space and then waved his free arm.

"Think, now, of the assignment and of what you want to portray," Millard intoned.

"Yes," Jacques said. He furrowed his brows and looked off into space. "I'm thinking."

Millard paused, "Now think of the concept coming toward us. Do you feel it, Jacques; can you see it coming towards us?"

"I do. I do," Jacques said.

Millard leaned over and talked softly into Jacques ear.

"It's here," Millard said, "and you see it."

"Not yet," Jacques said. "There's fuzz around it."

"I can see it," Millard said, "you must shoot me as … as … as a dangling participle!"

"Aha! Yes! That's it!" Jacques screamed. "Now the interior concept meshes with outer reality. I can do it!"

Jacques ran off.

"I don't know what the hell this all about," Binky said, "but if you don't shut the hell up and get that picture taken we're in big trouble. Let's do it and run the hell out of here."

"Gotcha," Millard said. "Believe me, I'm with you."

Millard sat in front of an off-white screen with a single spot background. His left side was highlighted. Jacques took three shots from a box camera at a little above eye level. Millard recognized the set and lighting as the same as every picture ever shot by any school photographer he'd ever faced.

-But what the hell, Millard told himself, it isn't often one teases banality out of Bedlam.

"What kooks, what a bunch of kooks," Binky muttered all the way to the St. Moritz. Millard sat back in the cab and let Binky bluster. Millard was tired; he felt he'd been running on a treadmill.

-I'm like one of those little white rats on a wheel that just keeps going round and round, Millard told himself.

The St. Moritz doorman greeted Binky and Millard with a nod. He looked askance at Binky's attire and noticeably sneered at Millard's. When Binky told the desk clerk their names, the desk clerk beamed and handed them two cards.

"What's this?" Binky asked.

"Your keys," the desk clerk said.

"They look like cards," Millard said.

The desk clerk sniffed and explained the St. Moritz had long abandoned keys. Every door was now operated electronically and a specific room could only be opened by a specific card with identical codes. He also explained the computer changed lock and card codes at random as a further security measure.

"Wonderful," Binky said.

"Clever," Millard said. But he missed the huge brass keys hotels used to issue.

"Look," Binky said to the desk clerk, "might we change the name of our suite to the Millard Fillmore Suite?"

The desk clerk paused and twirled his mustache. "I think that might be arranged."

"Thanks," Binky said and he took the cards and walked to the elevators.

The cards admitted Binky and Millard into a spacious and opulent suite. Millard walked around and investigated. A bank of windows overlooked Central Park; the bed was canopied; gold dolphins turned water on and off; the tub was sunken.

"Plush," Millard commented.

Binky sat in a chair by the telephone.

"Beats the West Side 'Y', doesn't it?" he asked.

"For sure," Millard said.

Binky picked up the phone. He waited. "Room Service," he asked. Again, he waited. "Room Service? Send two filets up to the Millard Fillmore Suite," Binky clapped his hand over the mouthpiece. "How do you want yours, Millard?"

"Medium."

Binky uncovered the mouthpiece. "Cook one medium and one rare. And some wild rice.. no? Well, rice pilaf will do, OK? And two baked potatoes with sour cream, two Caesar salads, come Camembert and a magnum of champagne. What? Oh, any Dom will do… let the wine steward choose. That's it. Got it? Fine." Binky replaced the phone in its cradle and sat back and sighed.

Millard wandered around in the suite. He finally alighted on the bed and rested. Binky lit a cigar and smoked; he was unusually quiet.

"It's going to be great," Binky chanted now and then and Millard nodded and waited for the food.

When the meal arrived, Binky and Millard ate greedily. Neither realized how hungry they'd become. There wasn't much talk. After the meal, Binky got up and put on his coat.

"Sit tight tonight, Millard," he said. "When the clothes come, we'll be going out a lot. Rest up. If you need anything, call Room Service. You pay in plastic so don't worry."

"I feel caged," Millard said.

"Yeah, but it's gilded," Binky said.

"True," Millard said.

"I'll be here tomorrow at seven," Binky said,"with the troops."

"What troops?"

"Media coaches."

"Media coaches?"

"Sure. You have to learn to talk, to walk and how to handle yourself in front of TV cameras. We'll drill you on a few routines."

"Wonderful."

"It's going to be a busy day."

"Yeah. Sounds it. Binky?"

"Yes?"

"What are you doing about your regular job?"

Binky smiled. "I took leave and farmed out my territory to some friends. It's OK."

"I take leave after sick time," Millard said, "only it was forced."

"Yeah," Binky said. "Me too." He opened the door. "Rest up. Enjoy. I'll see you later." Binky let himself out and shut the door. Millard walked to the windows and looked into Central Park.

-This isn't happening, he told himself. But he knew it was.

Millard watched television on a screen as big as a wall and then went to bed. Before going to sleep, he called Ethel.

"Hello," she snapped.

"It's Millard."

"What do you want?"

"How's it going?"

"How do you think?

"I don't know. I called to ask."

"It isn't easy being the wife and children of an international sex maniac."

"C'mon," Millard said. "I took one lousy blue pill."

"Do you care, Millard? Do you care about us?"

"Of course I care." There was silence on the other end of the line. "Ethel, I called to tell you I've moved from the 'Y'," Millard said.

"I suppose you're shacked up with some high-class chippie."

"No," Millard said, "I'm at the Millard Fillmore Suite in the St. Moritz."

"Now where are we going to find money for that?"

"A lot has happened. It's free. Don't worry."

"I'll bet."

"I lost my job, or, at least I'm on leave. Binky's my agent. We've incorporated. I've signed book and product endorsement contracts and we're mounting a campaign."

"What's her name?"

"Who?"

"This campaign you're mounting."

"Ethel, please," Millard pleaded. "I'm telling you things are going well."

"For you, maybe, but not for us. We can't hold our heads up in this neighborhood because of you. Your son got locked in his school locker with a package of condoms, you know."

"OK, Ethel, I give up," Millard said. "I wanted you to know where I was and what's happening."

"Thanks for nothing."

"'Bye," Millard said.

"'Bye," Ethel said.

Millard sighed, rolled over and went to sleep. He dreamed he was a subordinate clause in search of an active verb that wore a paisley beret. All night he went from conjunction to conjunction and knocked on doors in this frantic hunt. He awakened early in a fully blown panic because he'd wandered into a foreign land of punctuation and found himself chased by a multi-starred man-eating asterisk. It was awful. Millard had to order hot toddies with double gin chasers from room service just to get back to sleep.

# Viagro 5

For the next few weeks, Millard's life was not his own. Binky, or some agent under his command, led Millard from one assignment to the next. When there were no assignments, there were coaching conferences, posing practice, acting lessons, grooming lectures, picture taking and the recording of radio and TV commercials. Binky also hired an Indian guru so Millard would, in his words "apprehend the essences." Millard never got around to one single essence because the guru was rather child-like and giggled a lot and he and Millard spent their time playing"Space Invaders." The game pleased the guru immensely and Millard liked to see him laugh. The guru, who Millard called Wendell when they were alone, took particular pleasure in blasting invaders into electronic blips. He told Millard he thought the real invaders were "the damn Buddhists" who were "stuffed all full of cosmic shit." And, after he imparted this wisdom, Wendell would blip them into infinity and giggle. Millard was so busy he had no time to think and, since there was no time, Viagro didn't trouble him. Millard was glad about this.

 The frenetic period started with a follow-up interview with Nathan Guilder. The focus of the second Enquirer article was the dramatic change Millard's condition, and the National Enquirer's coverage of it, had made in Millard's life. The headlines read: "Man Rises To Occasion As Celebrity Status Hardens." Other print media interviews followed. Some were cute ("Teddy Roosevelt said, 'Walk softly but carry a big stick,' and his advice today is being taken by one Millard Fillmore...."). Some were serious ("Doctors at the Cryptic Institute of Phenomenology discussed today the probable cause of Millard Fillmore....").

Millard routinely got cited by newspaper editorial writers. He became a subject for three days in Gary Trudeau's "Doonesbury" cartoon. His name appeared as a staple in most of the personal columns ("Educated and fun-loving man in low forties with Millard Fillmore Syndrome seeks hedonistic teenager of just about any sexual persuasion...Bright, articulate and artistic NYC professional woman desires former sheepherder with a Millard Fillmore...Westchester threesome needs a Millard Fillmore perform-a-like...Submissive young man yearning for a master like Millard Fillmore...Winsome lass dreams of Millard Fillmore in a rubber suit...Elderly couple with large energy-efficient and temperature-controlled medieval chamber searching out a Millard Fillmore...Young couple into whips and chains needs a Millard for serious instructions...Do you like leather, Millard Fillmore?...Retired dancer with plastic water bed and unlimited supplies of Mazola wants to message you, Millard Fillmore...Bright, attractive, educated and liberated Tea Queen hopes Millard can Fillmore...." And, strangest and foggiest of them all, "There's a huge sack of granola ready for us both, Millard Fillmore....").

As the ink spread widened, Binky and company kept it fresh. The original plan worked well; Millard was first featured in the tabloids, then in men's magazines. His book and equipment advertisements were placed to maximize exposure. The first break in the legitimate press came from the New York Times. It could not ignore mention of Millard's book on the bestseller lists. As the book moved up, Millard drew attention from the alternative press, culminating with a thoughtful piece in The Village Voice that examined him both as a man and as a cultural symbol. The next notice appeared in the Wall Street Journal. Ben and Myron merged their Millard Fillmore lines with Millard Fillmore, Inc. and applied to an investment firm to go public. Binky told

Millard Ben and Myron had no real intention of floating stock but the application itself caused a spate of published reports. Finally, the New York Times featured Millard Fillmore as a "cultural icon." The article and pictures bought and sold the "respectable" image Binky and his advisors had worked to maintain. During the Times interview, Millard felt in full control. The training and coaching clicked and his performance was, in Binky's word, "flawless." After the Times article appeared, Binky called a conference at The Millard Fillmore Suite. All concerned parties were present. Millard was amazed at the number and variety of firms involved in his promotion.

"OK," Binky said as he opened the meeting, "we've done well so far. Everything's gone as planned and come up roses and Phase I is over. Now's the time for Phase II and munching of the Big Enchilada."

A chorus of assenting "ummms" greeted Binky's statement and the men nodded. Millard nodded just to be sociable.

"Phase II," Binky continued," as we all know, is the electronic phase. We get to light up the TV screens with this one."

Millard didn't know exactly how this would be accomplished but he chuckled and then looked solemn and tried to look wise as he had been instructed to do whenever he was puzzled. Since he was puzzled most of the time, this expression had had the most practice and was the most effective. Millard could look wiser than just about anybody.

"And I'm proud to say," Binky went on, "we've booked Millard on the Merv Griffin Show! This is the top talk show around except for Johnny. How 'bout that? The guys at William Morris are on the ball, say what?"

Murmurs of approval skittered around the room. It wasn't hard to find the guys from William Morris, they were looking down and shy and proud. Millard just looked wise.

"It's the start, the start of Phase II," Binky said,"and if we can meet here in a week or ten days with Merv, Mike, Phil and Johnny under our belt, we're in Phase III no problem."

Myron and Ben chomped their cigars and clapped wildly and guffawed and snorted and one or the other of them farted. The other men clapped politely. Millard thought it an odd mix…the boys with money looked crude and the boys making money looked slick.

"What's Phase III?" Millard asked.

Binky laughed. The other men laughed. Ben and Myron snorted.

"Phase III, Millard, is take the money and run Phase."

Everybody but Millard thought that funny so he watched them laugh and tried looking wise.

"OK, now, we've got to plan talk show strategy with specific guidelines for the Merv Griffin appearance," Binky said. "I suggest we take off our coats, roll up our sleeves and order some Scotch from Room Service and get to it."

Obediently, the men took off their coats and rolled up their sleeves and called for the booze. Ben called Room Service and the session began. Millard grew bored rather quickly. There was, for him, only so much romance in the argument of how or whether he should cross his legs on camera. However, the subject of gaffing his crotch interested him. It was brought up by one of the PR consultants.

"I have a concern, here," he began, "that arises out of this leg-cross controversy."

"Yes?" Binky said.

"It has to do with gaffing," the PR man said.

"Gaffing? What the hell is gaffing?" Binky asked. A look of surprise came over most of the faces and especially those of the lawyers and accountants.

"Gaffing is stuffing the crotch area with a towel," the PR man explained.

"Why do we have to think about that?" Binky asked.

"Look," the PR man said, "bullfighters gaff themselves with bath towels. These guys fight bulls that are symbols of masculinity, the very measure of virility. They can't go out looking all puny. It's the same with our guy here. He can't go out looking puny."

"So they stuff a towel in their pants?" Binky asked. "Fancy that."

"Sure," the PR man said, "at the firm we've had a lot of discussion about this but we wanted to wait to bring it up in Phase II, that is now, because Phase II is primarily visual."

"I like it," Myron said.

"Sounds good," Ben said.

"What's a good gaff cost?" an accountant asked.

"I'll have to research any and all pertinent gaff law," a lawyer observed. "We could get cited for fraud if Millard ain't hung like a horse."

Binky waved his hand. "Millard, what do you think?" Binky asked. "You're the one stuffing the towels?"

"Well," Millard said, "I've never given it much thought, except of course at the ballet where I always wondered how these little flitty guys were hung so huge you could serve a TV dinner on their dong."

"We think he'd best be gaffed," the PR man said, ignoring Millard deliberately, "and especially on TV."

"Hey," Binky said, "you were the guys who pushed the dignity approach. In fact, you were the ones who came up with it. How come now you want to do this? It's crude. And doesn't it fly in the face of what we're trying to achieve in terms of image?"

"Flies in the face, that's good, Bink," Millard said. Most laughed but the PR man did not laugh because they were not flippant about earth shattering decisions such as stuffing one's crotch full of towels.

"OK," said the PR man, "make jokes if you want but this is serious. We're selling a product here that is unseen. Credibility is essential. We only have Millard's word for his erection and some vague doctor's reports filched by The Enquirer…that I remind you nobody's seen or read. We think we've got to make a visual statement; we have to provide a tangible clue. Gaffing does it."

Binky frowned. The other men frowned. "He's got a point," Binky said. He nodded. The other men nodded.

"I don't want to stuff a bath towel in my crotch," Millard said. "It's dishonest. Besides, girls get kicked out of the Miss America contest for antics like that with their bosoms."

"Oh, c'mon," Binky said, "what's the alternative? You going to flash on national TV? You going to take your Brooks Brothers raincoat on stage and then go 'whoa-a-a-a-ah!' and poke the whole country?"

"No," Millard said.

"Or you want us to take a picture of the real thing and leak it?" Binky asked. Even Binky winced at this one.

"No!" Millard said. "John Holmes I'm not."

"I don't know how you're hung," Binky said, "and nobody here really cares but if we leak a picture of your hard-on to the press then you're in competition with monster cocks like John Holmes and pretty much in the same place image-wise."

"Actually," the PR man cut in, "we've researched Medieval English cod pieces and maximum effect can be achieved simply."

"How simply?" Millard asked. "I'll be damned if I'm going to wear cod. Fish doesn't keep well down there, you know. Nobody I know who fishes stuffs their pants with their catch to take it home."

"Yeah, right." the PR man said, "you have got to stop dicking around here. The cod, as it were, is a pretty simple piece."

"I haven't had a piece yet," Millard complained. "We're talking major omission."

"Wait a minute," Binky interjected, "I thought we're talking fish here."

"A cod piece! A cod piece!" the PR man yelled. "It has nothing to do with fish!"

"Then why did you tell my client he had to stuff a cod in his pants? So, just why don't you like towels, you got something against our good friends the Cannon and Wamsutta people?" Binky asked.

"I didn't say that," the PR man said.

"Yes, you did," Millard said.

"Are we selling fish or what?" Ben asked.

"I don't know," Myron said, "I'm still wondering how those little bullfighters get a whole bath towel to fit down into those skinny little sequined pants."

"I didn't name the sons-of-bitches," the PR man exclaimed, "the English did."

"Good," Binky said, "we've got it straight. Now what about my client?"

"OK," Millard said, "tell me how it can be done…how it can be simply done."

The PR man fell silent. "Oh, go stuff a hand towel for all I care," he murmured. "I give up."

"That's it? A hand towel?" Binky asked. "We're down to a hand towel? What about a wash cloth?"

"Folded right and placed right, it could do the trick," the PR man said.

"How much are hand towels?" the accountant asked. "Can anybody get them wholesale?"

"Jesus," the lawyer said, "I'm not sure there's any case law on gaffs and cods are fish and that would be in the maritime area. Hell, we don't have any maritime law specialists in our office."

"Shut up, you dolts," Binky roared. He arose, walked to the bathroom, ripped a hand towel off the rack, returned and threw it to Millard. "Problem solved," he declared. "Stuff this and shut up." He sat.

"What'll I do with this?" Millard asked.

"Stuff it," Binky growled. Millard laughed. Myron laughed. Ben laughed. The PR man looked glum. The accountant took out his picket calculator. The lawyer drummed his forehead with his fingertips and murmured "Gaffs and cods…gaffs and cods" over and over to himself. "OK," Binky said, "let's get on to the Merv Griffin Show."

Some days later, as Millard waited to go on the Merv Griffin Show, he had towel trouble. It kept slipping around and creating unconvincing bulges in all the wrong places. Binky went frantic and called the PR firm to double check the prescribed folding. By the time they got it right, Millard was frazzled and Binky was bent.

"Hey," Millard said, "what's the name of the book I wrote?"

"Nobody briefed you?" Binky asked. Millard shook his head. "Lord," Binky said, "I think it's 'Joy Uber Alice…The Great Sex Blast Off…' or something."

"You don't know?"

"No."

"Did you read it?"

"No."

Millard panicked. "I haven't read it either. I'm going out to plug my book on national television and I don't know its title or what's in it. This is crazy."

"Relax," Binky said." I thought one of Myron's boys had briefed you. It'll be OK. Merv never reads either. Just wing it."

"How? How the hell can I do that?" Millard blurted. He was next to tears.

Binky looked around and drew Millard aside. It wasn't necessary because they were alone in the Green Room. "It'll be OK," Binky said quietly. "Lots of celebrities come on this show and their books have been ghostwritten. They haven't read it either. They don't know what they wrote. You're not alone."

"But…," Millard protested.

"Shush," Binky said, "I'm coming to the good part."

"Yes?" Millard asked.

Again, Binky looked around and hushed his voice.

"The good part is that Merv's audience doesn't read, either. He never reads books and his audience doesn't either. It doesn't matter what you say."

"What?"

"Nor his staff. None of them. Somebody just skims the table of contents or opens it at random. Nothing big. Remember, they don't know what's in it either."

"Oh, thank god," Millard said.

"So you're home free," Binky said.

"But the title," Millard pleaded, "I at least have to know the title."

"Oh, hell," Binky said, "Merv's got to have a copy on the desk. Read it then. Or, if you miss it, you can read it when he holds it up to the camera. You can catch the title on the monitor. Not to worry."

With that assurance, Millard was whisked onstage.

"We have with us today," Merv said, "a man who's written a dynamite new book…" He held the book up to the camera, turned it toward himself and read the title. "…called 'Getting Yours' that is skyrocketing to the top of the charts." Merv flashed a winning smile, raised his eyebrow and cocked his head while flicking his tongue lightly through his front teeth. "…and the man who's really getting his all over the place, the man who wrote it, the man blessed by nature in a very unusual way…." Merv smiled broadly and the audience tittered. "I'm sure you've read of him. Will you please welcome, Mil-lard Fill-more!"

Millard walked onstage with the help of a quick push. He greeted polite applause. He wore his coat open and smoothly twisted his gaff to the camera as he had been taught. He walked easily up to Merv Griffin, smiled and shook his hand. He'd worked weeks on that. Then he flashed his gaff again and waved at the audience that responded with more applause. Suddenly, the band broke out with, "Yes, We Have No Bananas." Millard waited patiently but Merv looked mocking and disgusted. Jack Sheldon played the lead melody trumpet line and poured his heart out the end of his trumpet in a stirring melodic riff. Merv waited and then waved the band silent and again looked disgusted.

"Hey," Merv shouted, "can't you guys come up with a better song than that?"

Jack Sheldon grabbed the microphone.

"I wanted to do 'Some One of These Days'," he quipped.

The audience laughed and Merv looked pleadingly into the camera.

"Don't encourage him," Merv said. He turned to the band. "You could have played something else."

"Ray wanted 'Down By The Old Mill Stream'," Jack said.

Ray lifted his bass bow and tried to swat Jack with it. Jack ducked. Merv waved an arm of dismissal to the band.

"I'm sorry," he said to Millard. "They haven't been fed yet. The zookeeper's late."

"It's OK," Millard said. He looked dignified and amused as he had been coached.

"Is it true what they say?" Mrs. Miller croaked from the audience.

"What's that, Mrs. Miller?" Merv asked.

"Is it true what they say?" Mrs. Miller repeated only this time the camera was turned on her. Then the camera switched to Merv.

"What do you mean?" Merv hedged.

"I want to know," Mrs. Miller rasped. It was a zoom close up shot. The audience clapped.

Merv looked around and waited. "Yes," he said. The women in the audience squealed. The men clapped. Again, Merv waited. "It's true Mr. Fillmore wrote a book."

"Oh-h-h-h-h," the audience groaned. Merv smiled devilishly.

"Excuse all this," Merv said as he took Millard by the arm and led him to a seat. He mugged back at the audience in fake displeasure. Millard sat down and, as he did so, he opened and closed his legs and flashed his gaff. The drum rolled and a cymbal crashed. Merv glared at the band and sat down. Then he looked sincere.

"This is the most wonderful book I've ever read," Merv said. "How did you do it?"

"I...," Millard began.

"I've read books and I've read books but I've never read a book like I've read this book," Merv said.

"Thanks," Millard said, "I can tell..."

"It's a blockbuster, folks," Merv said, "and destined to become an American classic."

Shelley Winters, lead guest, sat quietly through all this but as Merv threatened to show the book on camera for the second time and end the interview she came alive.

"Hey, boy," she called down from her seat on Merv's far right, "are you doing anything for dinner tonight?"

"Me?" Millard responded, "No, I…"

"Now, now Shelley," Merv said and he shook a finger at her.

"I'm like every other American woman, Merv," she said, "I'm tired of spaghetti and I'm looking forward to a fresh big stick of hot salami."

The audience roared. Even Merv laughed. When the merriment died, Merv turned to Millard. Millard crossed and uncrossed his legs and looked dignified, yet pleased. He also acted a bit complimented. Feigning modesty, he glanced at Shelley to show his own interest. Finally, he looked embarrassed. The last was easiest. He was embarrassed.

"Cool it, Kitten," Merv said. He returned to the interview. "You've written a wonderful book," Merv said.

"Thank you," Millard said.

The audience settled back in their seats.

"Where you from?" Merv asked.

"Ohio," Millard said.

The band struck up "Beautiful Ohio" and then segued into the "Buckeye Fight Song."

"You guys could have played that first," Merv called.

"We thought maybe he was from Cleveland and then we'd have played 'Fire Up A Lazy River'," Jack called back.

The audience chuckled at the reference to Cleveland's being the only city with a river that caught fire. Merv, sensing the quick death of this joke, continued.

"It must have been hard growing up in Ohio," Merv said.

Jack Sheldon tooted a siren. The drum rolled and there were cymbals and a rim shot. Shelley screamed. Mrs. Miller threw her hotel key up on stage. Merv looked flustered. The audience careened out of control.

"Oh, no," Millard said when the din died, "growing up in Ohio was pleasant."

"And you wrote a book," Merv said. Millard could tell Merv was grasping for control.

"Yes," Millard said, "we tried to present the material tastefully, especially the pictures."

"You know," Shelley blurted, "spaghetti isn't so bad if there's sauce on it. It needs spices and plenty of sauce, don't you know?"

"Shelley!" Merv hissed. She sat back and chuckled to herself.

Millard snatched a look at the book on the table. "'Getting Yours' is meant to be guide and reference," Millard said, reading sales copy on the back of the book, "it's a treasure of the publishing art to give pleasure for a lifetime, a volume to be held and cherished forever."

-Whew! Millard thought, the important speech delivered.

"Oh, that's moving," Merv said, "moving and deep and heavy. We've kidded around here but the fact is 'Getting Yours' is a serious book, tastefully done and available now at your bookstore." Merv held the book aloft for the camera. "I urge you all to buy this so you can get busy getting yours for damn near forever." Merv's eyes glistened with sincerity and he patted Millard's knee affectionately." And written by a fine gentleman here who's remarkable condition made him the authority for all the rest of us." Merv replaced the book on the table and turned to Millard. "Thank you for coming," he said.

"You don't know that," Jack Sheldon cut in, "at least not for sure."

Shelley hooted. "I can check that out." Cymbals crashed. Ray pronged his bass. Jack blew a trumpet fanfare. Mrs. Miller threw diapers on stage. The audience tore off the backs of their seats. Merv dropped his head on his desk during all the commotion and then lifted it and smiled.

"That's it for today, ladies and gentlemen. I'd like to thank our guests, Shelley Winters, our resident spaghetti noodles gourmet; The

Fried Meat Band; oral surgeon Wendall Butcher, renowned spelunker; economist Moshe Blathered and his latest doomsday prediction; armchair philosopher and retired middleweight Rockno Pignatelli; Bertha and her trained slugs; impressionist cinematographer Hop Toad Warter whose interpretations of celebrities sleeping blazes new trails in the art of snooze; and author and sexpert and all around good sport, the honorable Millard Fillmore. That's it. G'night, ever'body." The band struck up the show theme and the cameras cut to commercials.

Once the Griffin interview aired, Millard soon graced the cover of People magazine. There he was heralded as a sedate, conservative, sexual guru whose book and line of sex aid and appliance offerings were "valuable contributions" to American culture.

The People spread triggered another ripple in the press. The Village Voice, The Times and the Wall Street Journal re-evaluated the first articles. Time, Newsweek and US News and World Report remarked on what they called "The Millard Fillmore Phenomena." Phil Donahue used Millard as a panelist in a couple of talk shows and Mike Douglas and Johnny Carson appearances followed in quick succession.

However, the Carson interview triggered the inevitable backlash. It was a total disaster. The flap sprung from this exchange:

"...Ah-h...," Johnny said, "I was wondering, Millard, if you were banned in Boston?"

"Beg pardon?" Millard asked.

Carson drew back. He looked surprised. "Of course." He turned to Ed McMahon. "Isn't it traditional, Ed, or didn't it used to be traditional, that a mark of success in books of this sort was to be banned in Boston?"

"Yes," Ed said, "you are correct, sir. But that was before they had a world class Combat Zone."

"Aha," Johnny exclaimed, "you're drunk again, aren't you Ed? So I put it to you, Millard..." Ed guffawed and the audience roared. "I was wondering, Millard," Johnny rephrased and continued, "have you, yourself, been banned in Boston?"

"I don't know," Millard replied. He grew nervous because he'd been briefed to sidestep moral questions and dealing with drunken Ed wasn't in his script. "I haven't received a notice."

Johnny turned to Ed.

"Does Boston give notice when it bans?" Johnny asked Ed.

"I don't know," Ed said, "I never saw one."

"Oh, sure," Johnny said, "They give notice or something. I've seen them. They say 'banned in Boston'."

"I never noticed a notice," Ed said and slapped his knee. He seemed only little drunk.

The drum rolled. The audience groaned. Ed laughed. Johnny looked innocent and surprised.

"Maybe they stopped noticing bans," Ed said, "or maybe they did notice and then they stopped it. It's the age for cutbacks, you know."

"Oh," Johnny said. He smiled and turned and mimicked drinking a quick shot when Ed wasn't looking. When Ed looked back he nodded as if he were thinking. "But they could do proclamations, though. They don't cost much. Lotsa cities do that." Ed looked pleased with himself but slightly puzzled. Johnny turned back to Millard. "Did you get a proclamation, Millard?"

"No," Millard said, "nothing. No notice. No proclamation."

"Well," Johnny said, "I think every American city ought to issue something."

"How 'bout a visa?" Ed asked.

"You're drunk, Ed, but that's good. that's very good," Johnny agreed. "It might show intent of some sort, perhaps even an intent to ban. Now Millard, has Boston refused you a visa, Millard?"

"No," Millard said. "I didn't know you needed a visa in Boston."

"You hear this, Boston," Johnny shouted into the camera, "this man is free to invade your city in his present condition. In New York, he's just another pretty face. But think what he could do in Boston!"

"Hey," Ed said, "I think there's a Moral Majority up there in Boston which could throw up ramparts."

Johnny winced. "I know some of them throw up, Ed, and if you don't lay off the sauce, you're probably going to do that yourself. But ramparts? What's with the ramparts?"

"It's something one mans," Ed said and his words were now slurred and his eyes watered. "They are something to throw up. Or, sometimes, something to wave over."

"Wave over? How's that?"

"Sure," Ed said, "remember the song? It says: 'o'er the ramparts it waved' or it might be 'they waved'. I don't remember."

"What about the visa?" Johnny asked. "Have you got any more on that visa, Ed?" He was signaling the audience openly now. "Do the Bostonians put a song on their visa when they wave it over a rampart?"

"No," Ed said, "in this instance I think it was a flag that waved and ours if I'm not mistaken. But the city in question was not Boston."

"Oh?" Johnny sat for nearly a full ten seconds and stared into the camera while working his eyebrows fiercely.

"Ho-o-o-o kay," Johnny said at last, "I haven't understood anything for ten minutes here so let's get to it. Ed you say we want Boston to man the ramparts and shout, 'The Millards are coming. The Millards are coming' is that correct?"

"No," Ed said, "that's not right. We've just got Millard here."

"No?" Johnny asked. He shifted his seat in total perplexity. "Well, what then?"

Ed stopped and thought and the sweat poured from his brow as light flickered in and out of his eyes. One could tell he was demanding a mind on vacation come quickly back to work.

"It's Millard is coming or The Millards are coming. See?"

"Stop," Johnny said, "that is so lame. We've got too much going as it is. Ed, you've got to sober up. Besides, I know for a fact the Moral Majority can't spell."

"What?" Ed asked. This new piece of information completely befuddled him.

"Sure," Johnny said, "they print slogans, don't they?"

"Haw, true," Ed said.

"So I think they can swing on ramparts, OK?"

"Fine with me," Ed said. "A person's ramparts is personal. What did we say about ramparts?"

Johnny thought. "We throw up on them, and wave goodbye over them, right?"

"Right."

"I say we let the Moral Majority write a visa for Millard here, OK?" Johnny said. He turned to Millard. "It's hard to believe that a distinguished man like yourself is…is…"

"Banned in Boston?" Ed tried. He wanted very much to salvage something.

"No," Johnny said, "Boston will issue that necessary visa. The Moral Majority will throw up on the ramparts and we can let whatever wants to wave wherever they want to wave it and even Millard could go where he wants and do the same. Is that OK?"

The audience clapped. Bringing all this together was a feat only Johnny could perform.

"Or," Ed offered, refusing to quit, "we could put Millard here on the ramparts and then we'd have a man on the ramparts and the Moral Majority could exit without a visa and Boston could proclaim a notice for everything and we'd all learn how to spell."

"Would that work?" Johnny asked.

"I don't know," Ed said. "Have you forgotten Boston's mostly Catholic?"

"Not on your life!" Johnny exclaimed, "I haven't expended so much energy since I did Abbott and Costello's 'Who's On First' routine."

"Theirs was better," Ed said.

"I know," Johnny said, "but Costello didn't hit the sauce and delivered his lines on cue. I think we've got this as good as it's going to get for the first time out."

"Right," Ed said. For the first time since this all started, Ed looked at ease and it seemed he just might give it up.

Johnny looked at Millard and shrugged and Millard nodded. Millard didn't want to say anything because somehow in all this mess all the forbidden PR buzz words came out…all the buzz words he'd been warned against precipitating and the whole thing was sure to bring down fire from just about everybody.

"Ed," Johnny said, "we don't have any animals tonight, do we? I hate animals and, after all this, I don't think I could take one."

"No," Ed said, "the only thing we got left for tonight is a wild rampart."

"Don't start with me," Johnny said, "it's been a long night."

Ed held up his hands and shook his head and smiled. He almost fell off the chair.

"OK," Johnny said, "if you at home have made any sense of this, any at all, be sure to see your doctor in the morning. I sure haven't. Ed is going night-night now. Buy this book." Johnny waved it, held it for a close up on screen. "It's called 'Getting Yours' and our own Millard wrote it. It's a modern classic. I know we have gotten as much of yours as we all can stand for one night. But it's a good book, so go out and buy it. That's it, I guess. G'night…"

After the Johnny Carson disaster was aired, Millard Fillmore drew flak from The Moral Majority, the Roman Catholic Church, Presbyterians, Methodists and one reclusive Shaker who appeared from the forest to wave a red flag of outrage. Not a few Southern Baptist towns did, in fact, issue visas to ban Millard Fillmore. The brouhaha polarized sexual attitudes pro and con. The counter culture press heralded Millard as a proponent of sexual freedom and his persecution by some organized religions hailed him as yet another example of backward thinking. Conservative publications used Millard Fillmore as the starting point to rail against the liberals and the counter culture press. They brought charges of 'snail darter mentalities' against them all. At one point, Millard was asked to appear on Issues and Answers between William F. Buckley and Gore Vidal. On another occasion, he was asked to Face the Nation between the Reverend Jerry Falwell and Bob

Guccione. But nothing came of it. Millard's advisors recommended against these appearances on the basis Millard would be needlessly adding to the chaos and most importantly, if he were constantly sitting, his gaff would never show. They were content to let the furor rage and tried to capitalize upon it. Which was very hard because nobody knew what the hell was going on or what was said by whom and when. Ed couldn't help out. He was in rehab at the time.

All this time, Millard found himself less and less happy. There were lunches at Regine's where he grew fond of caviar-stuffed eggs and nights at Studio 54 where he danced with luscious young women. He gave cocktail parties at his suite where short bald men talked to him with cigars pointed at his chest and where women lapsed into psychobabble while offering odd critiques of unknown and obscure artists.

One evening at a cocktail party in the Millard Fillmore Suite a large and mannish woman arrived already strung out. She was escorted by a male venture capitalist who was at least six inches shorter than his date. Millard recognized him as a frequent cigar pointer. The woman, as she entered, first opened her eyes wide to adjust to the room light. Then she spotted Millard and walked toward him with fierce determination.

"Hey," she said, "you the host? You Millard?"

"Yes," Millard said, "may I get you a drink?"

"No," the lady said, "my name's Evelyn Poppe and I do those things for myself."

Evelyn looked around, spotted a drink tray, left, grabbed and glass and quickly returned.

"So," Evelyn said as she gulped her drink, "you're Millard Fillmore."

"Yes," Millard said.

Evelyn drew herself up to her full height. She was a foot taller than Millard and from this height advantage she glared down.

"What's your position on the Equal Rights Amendment?" Evelyn demanded.

"Don't have one," Millard said. "I'm not political."

"Of course you are," Evelyn said. "Living is a political act. Politics is life."

Millard smiled. "No," he said. "Not for me." He turned to leave. He could tell Evelyn was not only strung out and spaced but aching for a fight. Evelyn grabbed his arm.

"Look," Evelyn said, you're the one with the hard-on, right?"

"That's right," Millard said. He extracted his arm from her grasp with great difficulty. She was strong enough to throw the shot put.

Evelyn's voice grew louder. "Well, I want to know what a real prick thinks about the Equal Rights Amendment."

"Excuse me," Millard said. He moved to leave again. Evelyn's hand clamped hard on his arm. Other partygoers stopped talking.

"Don't you move, mister," Evelyn said, "I'm the holder of a pink belt in the martial arts and when I ask a question I want an answer."

"All right," Millard said, "I think ERA is super wonderful. That do it?"

"Not quite," Evelyn said. Evelyn's escort came up behind her and poked her in the back with his cigar.

"Evelyn, please," he said, "don't make a scene. This isn't a political rally. The days of radical chic are gone. The Black Panthers have largely disbanded."

"Evelyn turned, released Millard's arm, and threw a quick little left jab that landed neatly on her escort's jaw and exploded his cigar right up into his face. Stunned, he stood for only a moment and then fell flat on his back.

"Politics is life!" she screamed. The sight of the prone man laying face up with his splattered cigar clenched in his teeth, the cigar blooming out of his face like some huge and ragged brown flower, plus the scream, pretty much killed the rest of the party. Evelyn's voice then calmed to a menacing whisper. "Now, Millard," she hissed, "we live in the age of consumer protection and I want to see the merchandise."

"What?" Millard asked.

"The merchandise. I'm a consumer. I bought your book. You're marketing a hard-on. I want to see the goods."

"That's impossible," Millard said.

"Whip it out," Evelyn growled. "Show that sucker. As a consumer, I got rights. I want to see what I'm buying."

With that, Evelyn grabbed Millard by the shirt collar, picked him up with one hand and clawed at his belt. Millard could feel she was seriously disarranging the gaff. Binky ran up behind Evelyn and tackled her at the waist. Two other security men came up beside her and each took an arm and Evelyn had to release Millard who plopped back to the floor. The men quickly escorted Evelyn out.

"You've not heard the last of this," Evelyn screamed, "I'm filing a complaint with the Consumer Protection Agency."

Millard was ruffled, confused but unhurt. He tucked in his shirt and straightened his tie. He scrunched his pants to rearrange the gaff.

"You OK?" Binky asked.

"Yeah," Millard said, "but I think I'll call it a night."

Binky nodded. "Might as well. The crazy lady killed the party." Sure enough, Millard could see the guests drift out the door.

When Evelyn's escort revived, compliments of a glass of champagne dashed in his face, an act that seriously wilted his tobacco flower, he apologized and offered to pay damages.

"Normally," he said, "Evelyn's just another bull dyke feminist and a real sweetheart. But when she snorts a little too much, she thinks she's Queen Kong."

"That's OK," Millard said. He was tired and unhappy and wanted to go to bed.

"I gave her too much shit to sniff. It won't happen again."

"Sure," Millard said. "do try to keep her away from the AK-47's and the rocket launchers, OK?"

"Will do. Sniffing too much shit, that's all. My fault. Real sorry."

"Sure," Binky said while listing damages and toting up figures on his calculator. He hoped to give the man a bill on the way out. Binky also eyed Millard; he could tell he was out of sorts.

After the party Millard and Binky were alone. Binky tried to comfort Millard.

"It's OK," Binky said.

"Look," Millard said, "I'm tired."

Binky sighed. "Go on to bed then."

"No," Millard said, "you don't understand. I'm tired of this, of all of this. When does it stop?"

Binky scratched his head. "Not until the money stops," he said. "We're raking it in."

"I don't have a moment's peace," Millard said. "I have crazy persons honking my horn."

"You're just tired," Binky said. "You'll feel better in the morning."

Millard was unconvinced. And, when Binky left after delivering a stirring pep talk, Millard went to bed and was still unconvinced.

# Viagro 6

That night, Millard had trouble sleeping not only because Viagro broke a long silence but also because he uncorked a whole magnum of self pity.

=Hey, Turkey, Viagro said, remember me?

Millard sighed.

-Yes, Millard answered, how could I forget? I thought you'd left.

=Left, hell, Viagro said, I've just been keeping a low profile.

Millard rolled over.

=I'm still here, Viagro said, and I'm waiting.

-Waiting? Waiting for what?

=For the action. I've been waiting weeks for the action. I've made you rich. I've put you where the girls are. And what do you do? You go to acting lessons, motion lessons, diction lessons, photo sessions. It's enough to drive a poor prick nuts.

-Sorry, Millard said. I've been busy. And, if the truth were known, I'm glad this stuff pushed you out.

=Thanks a lot, Viagro said. You never were long on gratitude. But I'm not going to be pushed out any more.

-That a threat? Millard asked.

=No threat, Viagro said, a statement of fact. I'm back and I'm going to stay.

-That's all I need, Millard fumed. This whole plastic bag is coming down around my neck and now you're back to pull it tight around my neck and cut off my air.

=Hey, Viagro said, I'm unhappy, too. The plan was to get you in a position to do some good. And do you do me, or us, any good at all? Hell, no! You go to lessons and and conferences and parties where the most exciting thing that happens is you get ripped by a strung out bull dyke. What kind of life is that?

-I've been asking myself the same question, Millard said.

=I want you to get on the ball, here, Viagro said. Call room service and order a matched pair of hot and cold running maids.

-No, Millard said, this is the San Moritz.

=What the hell's that got to do with getting laid?

-This is a class joint.

=Watch your tongue! I'm a class joint. This is a hotel.

-OK, have it your way.

=Well-l-l-l, Viagro said, if you don't want to contribute to the bell captain's retirement fund, let's get dressed and stroll down Seventh Avenue. It's not too late for the hustlers to be out.

-I've checked them out, Millard said. They all have bad teeth. Have you noticed? Seventh Avenue hookers have bad teeth.

=You're not renting their dental work...

-I know. But it turns me off. The magic is gone.

=Magic? Magic? You're looking for magic in a Seventh Avenue streetwalker?

-No, Millard admitted, but there has to be something. Otherwise it's only lust.

=Lust you can get on Seventh Avenue. Magic you might get with a super high-priced call girl. She'll bring it along in a little plastic sack and sell you some and lend you her spoon.

-Oh, right.

=Your attitudes are strange. You give me a real hard-on, you know?

-Coming from you, that's quite a statement.

=You know what I mean, Viagro groused.

Millard got up, put on his bathrobe and wandered to his window. Once there, he looked out over the city. He felt discontented and very much alone. Then Millard heard something. He didn't believe it at first because it started softly. He thought it might be coming from another room or from down the hall. It was a sniffling sound. And, as it grew louder. Millard knew there was no mistake. Viagro was crying. Millard stood at the window in surprise and shock. This wasn't like Viagro. He'd always been crude and rude and tough. The sounds grew louder and he could tell Viagro was sobbing away, way down there in his pants.

-What is this? Millard asked himself.

Viagro didn't answer. Viagro sobbed louder.

-I hurt your feelings, or what? Millard asked.

But Viagro went on crying.

"Look,"Millard said aloud, "stop this. Tell me what's wrong!"

The sound of his own voice skittering around the suite startled him.

=It's…It's…" Viagro tried between snuffles.

"Go on!" Millard commanded.

=It's hard being a hard-on with no place to go. It's really hard, I tell you."

-You're telling me?" Millard thought.

=It's true, Viagro weeped. And it's no joke, either! I've done my job, worked hard, kept silent all this time and for what? For what? To sit in some lousy hotel room while life goes on all around me. And you, you gutless lackluster nerd, you sit around and tend your money tree while I wait and wait and wait and nothing happens.

-This isn't a lousy hotel, Millard countered. It's the San Moritz.

=Moritz, Schmoritz! What do I care? I'm starving to death, being denied and ignored and frustrated. I tell you I want to throw up the windows and shout, 'I'm mad as hell and I'm not going to take it any more!'

-That's been done, Millard said. It was in a movie.

=Yeah?

-They did that in "Network."

=Well, it's a damn good idea no matter where I stole it from.

-Get serious. You can't wave out the window. You'd get arrested.

Viagro grunted and then lapsed into little baby sniffles that filled Millard with compassion and tenderness. You would, he corrected Millard.

-Look, Millard said, maybe things will change. Maybe things will get better.

Viagro groaned.

=Only you can make it better and you won't, Viagro wailed.

-Hey, Millard said, you knew what I was when you first came around.

=I wanted to change all that.

-Right. And you have. Kind of. But any real change is up to me, not you. I change me; you change you. It's a law.

=Oh-h-h-h, Viagro groaned, I could die. I could just die. I want to shrivel up and die!

The statement frightened Millard. The thought of Viagro leaving panicked him. Where would he be? What would he do? He would really be in trouble.

"Now look," Millard said aloud, "I'm not sure how a penis commits suicide but I'm damn sure you can shrink up and go away if you want. I've had enough crazy talk for the night and we'd both better go to bed here and take another look at this in the morning…when we're fresh."

=I could die, I tell you. I could shrivel up and die! I hope you go swimming in cold water!

"Stop that," Millard said firmly. "Tomorrow morning I'm getting us in to see Dr. Heatherton and we'll get some help for you. But for now, for tonight, we're going to sleep. And that's that!"

Viagro sniffled.

=Won't help, he groused. You're a chicken shit mofu.

-Give it a chance, Millard said. You can always shrivel up and die. Give it a chance. And stop that language.

Viagro sighed.

=OK, he said. I'll try.

-That's-my-boy, Millard thought.

And with that, he went back to bed and restlessly dreamed away what was the rest of the night.

"What's the emergency?" Dr. Heatherton asked. Millard noticed Dr. Heatherton looked as striking as ever. He walked around the office and read the diplomas and certificates. Then he sat in the chair and stared straight ahead. "I've been reading about you," Dr. Heatherton said. "Seems you've moved up in the world."

"Yes," Millard said, "I've a suite at the San Moritz; I dine at Regine's and dance at Studio 54. I also have an army of accountants, lawyers and consultants."

Dr. Heatherton looked at Millard carefully. "You don't sound happy about all this," she observed.

"It's OK," Millard said. Then he sniffed.

"And what about your wife?" Dr. Heatherton asked. "Do you see your wife and family at all?"

"No," Millard said. "We talk on the phone now and then. I embarrass her."

"Embarrass?"

"She says she can't hold her head up in the neighborhood…that sort of thing. I think she's readying a divorce. There are a lot of hungry lawyers in my neighborhood."

"Oh." Dr. Heatherton waited. Millard paused.

"I didn't come here about me," Millard said. "I came about Viagro."

Dr. Heatherton shifted in her chair and looked surprised.

"Let me understand this. You're seeking psychiatric help for your talking penis? Is that correct."

"Yes ma'am, I think he's depressed."

"You want me to talk to Viagro?"

"Yes," Millard said. "He's really in a bad way. I think he's suicidal. He's threatening to shrivel up and die."

"Aha," Dr. Heatherton said, "he's talking and threatening suicide?" She looked at her notes. "You said last time he talked but then he was crude and rude and you feared he was taking control of you…let's see…you said you were afraid he'd force you to do unwanted things. Is that now the case?"

"No," Millard said, "when all the hype started and I got busy, he went away. Or at least he was silent. I thought he left. But last night he came back. He was angry."

"Why?"

Millard hesitated and looked around furtively.

"Because I've given him no sex life. He says he just wants to die." Millard stood up in great agitation. "Look," he said, "can't you talk to him? He's the one who needs help!"

Dr. Heatherton leaned back in her chair and studied the situation.

"How do you propose we do that?" she asked. Millard sat down.

"I sit here and tell you what he says," Millard explained. "He's a voice in my head and I'll just say aloud what he says."

Dr. Heatherton's eyebrows arched.

"Oh?"

"Sure," Millard said, "we did it once before…for a short time. Remember?"

Dr. Heatherton sighed. She puzzled a while and then nodded.

"All right," she said. "If that's what you want. But we can't go on babying your delusions forever." She waited.

=Hi, Viagro said through Millard. Still got your ruler?

"Yes," Dr. Heatherton said, "but I don't think that's necessary any more."

=Damn, Viagro said, that was the real fun part of the visit.

"Millard tells me you're depressed?"

=It's true. It's time to get my ticket punched.

"Ticket?"

=Get out. Leave. Vacate. Gooooo-BYE!

"How do you do that?"

=I just shrivel up and poof.

"Is it that simple?"

=Yes. I disappear. That's all.

Dr. Heatherton paused. She picked up her pencil and doodled on her legal pad.

"Are you aware of how Millard feels about this?"

=Sure, Viagro said. He thinks it's scary. He wonders what will happen to him. I've been his meal ticket, you know."

"Is disappearing what you want?"

=All I ever wanted was to get laid. It's apparent Millard's not going to do anything about that. I've waited. I've worked to give him opportunities and what does he do? He lives like a virgin. What other man in his position would act like that? Not many. I'm disgusted and I've wasted my time. I'm leaving. At heart, Millard's lackluster. His father was right.

"This doesn't sound like suicide," Dr. Heatherton said,"this smacks of revenge."

=Yeah, Viagro said, it's like that. But I had to get Millard's attention, you know? I am going and I'm letting Millard believe I'm going to join that Great Hard-on In The Sky. It's sort of revenge.

"Millard? Millard!" Dr. Heatherton called. "Are you with us? Did you hear?"

"Yes?" Millard said. He shook his head as if he'd been in a trance.

"Have you been listening?"

"Yes."

"Did you hear Viagro is leaving…not committing suicide?"

"Because I'm lackluster," Millard said. "He said it was because I was lackluster." Millard's eyes puddled up. "Cruel bastard."

"It's all right" Dr. Heatherton said,"we can work this out."

Millard sniffled.

"Now," Dr. Heatherton said, "when he leaves, can you handle it? He seems OK about it...but how about you?"

"I think so," Millard said. "In a way, I want it to happen..."

"Good."

"...and in a way, I don't. He was obnoxious at first...but tolerable. Now, he's not even tolerable. Yes. I hope he goes."

"Very good," Dr. Heatherton said, "and then you and I can work on other things."

"What other things?"

"Things. Like, say, why Viagro came, why he left, why he acted as he did, the whole lackluster thing..."

"Oh," Millard said. He got up to leave. "I've had enough for now. I'd like to go. Thanks for seeing us...me." He smiled. Dr. Heatherton smiled.

"Stay in touch," Dr. Heatherton called.

When Millard left the office of Dr. Heatherton, the receptionist spoke.

"Goodbye, Mr. President," she said.

"Yes, goodbye," Millard said. He was too tired to fight. But he also felt free for the first time in a long time. It was a good feeling and he walked with a spring in his step.

The next morning, Millard looked down and saw Viagro went flaccid. His penis was shrunken and scrunched up on his stomach. He no longer needed the tape. Millard ripped the tape off and watched with pleasure as his penis drooped into his forest of pubic hair and nestled back and hid away as usual.

"Wow!" he shouted. "It's over!" Millard stood and enjoyed the moment. Then he ran to the phone and called The National Enquirer. He asked for Nathan Guilder and waited as a series of clicks and transfers put him there.

"Nathan? Nathan?...Listen, it's me, Millard Fillmore...you want a scoop? Yes? OK?...My hard-on went away. Yes, it's true. It retreated. Left. Went poof. I've been cured. Dr. Susan Heatherton did it…Heatherton! Dr. Susan Heatherton! She's the shrink I've been seeing…you said you had documents from her office. No? No matter. I don't care…just print that it's over and I've been cured…You want the whole story? What happened from beginning to end? Hey, no problem. Come up then. But make it early…about nine thirty is good…See ya!"

Millard next called Binky Derth and told his answering service what he'd done with Nathan and when the interview was scheduled. Then he called room service and ordered steak and eggs for breakfast. Millard felt wonderful. He hummed and sang to himself as he waited for breakfast.

Binky soon arrived. He was all lit up and red and his face contorted in breathless panic.

"What have you done?" he screamed as he ran through the doorway of the suite. "What have you done!"

Millard munched his piece of steak.

"I went to the doctor yesterday. We talked. And this morning when I woke up the hard-on was gone. So I called Nathan Guilder."

Binky sat on the bed and his face went white.

"Why'd you do that?" he asked. "That's crazy. Why'd you do that?"

Millard cut into one of his eggs. The yolk broke and spread a bright yellow over the plate.

"Nathan broke the story," Millard said. "He has first right to report its end."

Binky wagged his head and tried to screw control into his face.

"'OK," he said, "damage control. Now when Nathan gets here, we'll tell him it's a ruse. That you lied. We'll tell him everything is OK, that you…ah…"

"No," Millard said. "We'll tell him what I told him we were going to tell him. I'm cured and it's all gone."

Binky grew super agitated and jumped up and paced the floor and gestured wildly.

"We can't do that," he said. "We've got a pile of cash riding on this and we can't pull out now. We'll lose everything. We'll tell Nathan you had a momentary mental lapse but it's all right now."

"No," Millard said. His tone was measured and firm. Binky studied Millard's eyes for a moment.

"Mil-lard, Mil-lard," Binky pleaded, "think what you're doing. This information will close us down. It'll not only blow our image but we'll also take a financial bath."

"I don't care," Millard said, "I'm tired of all this. I want my life back. This is the way it is."

Binky sidled up to Millard and put his arm around his shoulder.

"We don't need to release this, not yet," Binky crooned. Millard shrugged. "What does the public care if you really have a hard-on or not? What's wrong with letting them believe you still have it? It's just a little longer. Then we can move away gracefully and cash all those lovely checks…"

"Can't do it," Millard said.

"Sure you can," Binky said. "We can deflect Nathan Guilder and say nothing about it. We'll give him some cock and bull story. We only need a couple of weeks and we can pull out with a real pile of cash."

"It's not going to happen that way," Millard said. He brushed his breakfast tray aside and threw his legs out of the bed and onto the floor. He strapped on his robe and walked to the window. "I'm glad it's over," Millard said. "This whole mess has ruined my life."

"Not so fast," Binky said. You can't bail out just like that."

"Why not?"

"There are others to consider. Myron and Ben are investing in inventories up to their eyebrows; the PR people are on the eve of a major ad splash; the lawyers are drawing up a bundle of contracts. Think of all these people. And yourself, too. How are we to pay for all this? How are we going to dodge all the law suits?"

"I've been meaning to talk to you about money," Millard said. "How much is there? What do we have?"

Binky sat down in a chair and looked at the floor.

"Right now," he said, "every penny we have is reinvested. If you pull out now, there's probably less than zero."

"Zero? Less than zero?"

Binky sighed.

"We'll get sued. And Myron and Ben will have to eat their inventories so they'll stick it to us." Binky shook his head. "What a mess." He looked at Millard. "If you could wait for two weeks, three at the most, we'd get out with our skins and then some."

"Can't do it," Millard said. "I'm sick and tired of the whole thing. The fact is…"

"The hell with facts," Binky screamed. "Facts aren't reality. Perception is reality. The public perception of you, not you, is reality. All the rest is shit."

"I can't believe that," Millard said.

"Yeah, with an attitude like that, you'll never vote Republican."

Millard raised his eyebrows. There was a knock on the door. Binky jumped up. He looked frantic.

"Don't do it. Don't do this," he pleaded.

Millard shrugged and walked to the door. As he turned his back on Binky, he heard a long moan.

Nathan Guilder switched on his tape recorder as soon as he stepped into the room.

"Hi, there, Millard Fillmore," he said into the machine. "What have you got for me?"

"Hi, Nathan Guilder," Millard also said into the machine.

Nathan waited. "Are we just going to stand here and talk into the box?" Nathan asked.

"I don't know," Millard replied, "you started talking into it first."

"So I did, "Nathan admitted.

Millard bent down to the box. "Come-on-in-Mr.-Guilder-and-sit-down," he said loudly, "you-are-always-welcome-here in-the-Millard-Fillmore-Suite-at the-San Moritz-hotel."

Nathan jerked the instrument away and walked into the room.

"C'mon," he said, "Don't get funny. I have to carry this…it's lawyer's orders."

"I see," Millard said.

Nathan spotted Binky. "Who you?" he asked.

"Binky Derth. Millard's agent," Binky said.

Nathan shrugged and sat down. "Tough break, sport," he said. He turned to Millard. "OK, Millard," he said, "spill it. What's the story? And talk so the little box can hear you."

Millard recounted his life from his first visit to the doctor to the present. He dwelt especially on the time required by promotion and conferences and coaches and lessons.

"In short, you didn't get laid," Nathan said. "Bottom line is, all this shit, and you didn't get laid."

"Not much," Millard admitted. He was too embarrassed to say he hadn't been laid at all.

"So the high life for you didn't have any…ah…luster?" Nathan asked.

"As for luster, it totally lacked," Millard said.

Nathan nodded. "That's good," he said. "We can use that one. That's a good lead into the story." Millard smiled. He was glad of the coaching that taught him to capitalize on words. He was particularly glad, for personal reasons, to make a play on the fateful word lackluster. "I think I got it," Nathan said. He snapped off the machine. Binky held his head in his hands. Nathan looked over at him and shrugged. "Anything else?"Nathan asked Millard.

"No," Millard said, "that is it."

"Anything from you?" Nathan asked Binky.

"Can you kill the story?" Binky asked.

"You got to be kidding," Nathan said.

"Can you hold it?" Binky asked, "for three weeks or so?"

"C'mon," Nathan sneered. He got up, shook hands and left.

When he'd gone, Binky started to cry. Little rivulets of tears trickled down his cheeks. "It's all over," he sobbed.

"Yeah," Millard said, "ain't that great?"

Binky frowned. "We'll have to close down the Millard Fillmore Suite," Binky said.

"When?" Millard asked.

"Now's good," Binky said.

"What! Now?" Millard exclaimed.

"Now,"Binky said, "pack your things. You don't think Myron and Ben and the other stockholders are going to sit still for this expense when an economic Dunkirk is days away, do you?"

"Guess not," Millard said, "so where'll I go?"

"That's your problem," Binky said. "You killed us. You should have thought of that when you blew yourself off and took us all with you. Also, I'm calling in your credit cards."

"Damn," Millard said."What'll I live on? I need money. Where's the money that's been piling up all these weeks?"

"Expenses," Binky mumbled. "Reinvestments. The golden weeks were just beginning."

Millard reached in his wallet and pulled out the credit cards. He tossed them into Binky's lap. "Some agent you are," he said.

"Some client you are," Binky replied. "You get one inch away from the brass ring and jump off the ladder." He sighed, reached in his pocket and pulled out some bills that he handed to Millard.

"You can use this petty cash file, sort of a little walking around money."

"Thanks," Millard said. Do I get to keep the clothes?"

"Sure," Binky said, "we've already depreciated them. Besides, second hand clothes don't bring much."

"Wonderful," Millard said.

"I'll be shutting down the whole operation," Binky said, "and trying to salvage any money. Keep in touch. I owe you a full accounting. If we don't get sued, there might be a dollar or two left."

Millard counted the bills in his hand. There was less than one hundred dollars.

"This won't keep me afloat for long," Millard said.

"I'll try to get you more," Binky said, "but I don't know where it's going to come from." He looked at Millard. "I'll try to tide you over; I really will," he promised. "Even though you are one stupid bastard."

"Thanks," Millard said. He didn't have much faith in Binky's promise. Binky sighed, got up and left. Millard went to his closet and put on a sport outfit. Then he tore a sheet from the bed, dumped his entire wardrobe and other belongings into it, wrapped it up and walked out. Once in the lobby, he tossed the key to the room clerk.

"The Millard Fillmore Suite is closed," he said. The room clerk looked up in surprise. "I'm checking out," Millard said. "You can bill the corporation."

"But...," the room clerk stammered.

"'Bye now," Millard said and he walked out with one bed sheet from the St. Moritz holding all his present possessions.

Millard looked up and down Central Park South. He wondered if he could set up in the park but he figured shopping-bag ladies would have claimed all the really nice spots. So he went to back to the West Side "Y."

The "Y" was hosting an American Youth Hostel convention. Bikes were everywhere; they were Krypton-clamped to the outside fence and stuffed into phone booths and tiered in the lobby. Millard had trouble getting to the check-in counter without getting his pants greased and oiled. The hostel riders were usually unaware of their surroundings...but those who were aware were definitely hostile. "Look out for the fucking machine, dad," one growled as Millard brushed a tissue thin chrome fender. Because of the convention, rooms were at a premium. Also, Millard had to explain his luggage. Being a member helped. Paying in advance helped. Standing near the checkout desk helped. Slipping the room clerk five dollars helped. He finally got a room on the seventh floor. It faced north. Millard sat on the side of his bed and thought about his predicament. He counted his money. He had less than sixty dollars. Millard tucked his room key in his pocket, went to the washroom and slapped water on his face. He then left the "Y", and headed downtown to Monmouth Insurance Company.

Once there, he caught the elevator to the executive suite. He barged past receptionists and security persons and walked unannounced into President Myron Blower's office. Myron did not turn around; he was staring at the library wall. As Millard drew closer, he saw that Myron had on a small pair of earphones. And. instead of staring at the library wall, he was staring at a particular shelf that hid a tape machine and a Sony color TV. Millard noted the doors that opened to expose the equipment were fake books. Myron smiled and nodded to himself. Millard had no trouble walking up behind Myron undetected. He looked at the screen. Linda Lovelace, the decade's reigning porn queen, walked through a park. She smiled coyly at a man walking a dog. The man was tall and only moderately good looking. The dog was a Black Labrador Retriever. Myron's secretary burst into the room.

"Mr. Blower is not to be disturbed," she said. Her face brightened as she recognized Millard.

Millard shushed her and motioned her forward. The secretary scurried up to where Millard stood. Myron went on nodding and smiling. The secretary parked beside Millard and also looked at the screen. Linda and the man in the park already were in the bedroom. They disrobed. The man took the collar off the dog. Linda looked lustfully at the man's penis that, at rest, was the size of a yardstick. He walked over to the dog and patted him. The dog got excited and ran around in circles with his huge pink tongue hanging out.

"Mr. Blower is in conference, Millard," the secretary said.

"I see," Millard said. He winked at her.

She sighed. On the TV screen, Linda grabbed the man's penis with both hands and stroked it. She watched wide-eyed and lusty as it grew larger and larger. She looked surprised, then pleased as it grew, and all the while she licked her lips. The man, however, showed more interest in the dog and while Linda was working, he called the dog to him. Then he talked to Linda in a very serious fashion. Linda didn't seem to like what he was saying and began her trademark sword-swallowing trick. While she was thus engaged, the man patted the dog and pointed to it and kept on talking and Linda, even with her mouth full, listened and shook her head and thought while she gobbled. It was obvious as she moved further and further down the shaft she warmed more and more to the idea of the dog thing. Even the dog got the hint and frothed more at the mouth and sported its own erection. When Linda was within a few inches of totally enveloping the yardstick, the man tried to stop her and the dog went bananas, Millard called out.

"Mr. Blower? Mr. Blower!" Millard shouted.

President Blower jumped forward in his chair and in a frenzy pushed hidden buttons under his desk. The fake doors snapped shut just as Linda, despite all obstacles, reached her final goal and was now trying to stuff two huge testicles into her cheeks. Myron turned around and ripped off his earphones. He saw he was discovered and looked sheepish and flustered and angry and embarrassed.

"Been looking at some projections," he stammered.

"It's no fun until Linda and the dog get on the trapeze," Millard said.

"I like the part with the skateboard," the secretary said. "I never saw anybody swallow a whole skateboard before."

"Ah-h-hem!" Myron cleared his throat.

"The part with the pony isn't bad," Millard said.

"The freefall with the dog is totally gripping," the secretary said.

"That'll be all," Myron said. His white mane of hair quivered and his red face glowed scarlet. The secretary left. "What can I do for you?" Myron asked Millard. Millard sat down.

"I'm ready to return to work," Millard said. "My…ah…problem has been cured. The Enquirer is going to print a story to that effect in its next edition."

"Aha! Yes. Well?" Myron said, "we're happy for you of course. And you? You happy about this turn of events?"

"Yes," Millard said.

"Good," Myron said, "now the board and myself have discussed this matter in depth. We feel resuming your career at this time, or at any time, is not in your best interests or in the best interests of Monmouth Insurance."

"Why not?" Millard asked. "I quote prime good. I have excellent job evaluations. You signed them yourself."

"Aha," Myron said, "that's true. We have no displeasure with your work. Our unhappiness is with your notoriety. We are a solid company and want to present solidity at all times. This is not what we want."

Millard fidgeted in his chair.

-But it is solid, he thought A hard-on is solid. They don't say got wood for nothing.

"Look, Myron," Millard said, "I'm broke and I need the job."

Myron's eyebrows lifted. "I should think you'd be well off by now."

"My agent's not so sure," Millard said. "There's been some creative accounting. Right now I have a cash flow problem and I'm broke."

Myron smiled. "We can help there," he beamed, "we've given you a generous severance allowance in anticipation you'll sign a waiver not to prosecute us in any fashion. That, plus your retirement account, your sick leave and vacation leave, and the cash out of your stock options should keep you going for literally weeks."

Millard leaned back in his chair and sighed. His old job had looked good to him. In fact, his old life looked good. Now it was over. He couldn't go back. He was sad.

"I like your suit," Myron noted.

"Brooks," Millard said. "Is that it? Is this all you can tell me?"

"That's it," Myron said. "The paymaster can cut your check by the time you get downstairs. Don't forget the waiver. It's a condition."

-I knew it all along, Millard thought, why did I try? He paused. I guess because I wanted it so much, he concluded.

Millard arose. "Thanks," he said, "you've been wonderful."

Myron beamed. "We at Monmouth are nothing if not fair."

"You know, Myron," Millard said, "This place is nothing. I've had a lot of experience in PR lately. And I've been thinking about that experience in relation to Monmouth."

"Yes?"

"And I think what this company needs is a spokesperson to capture its essence and to relate it to its customers."

"Go on."

Millard got up and walked around.

"I think this company needs a new public image, an image that can sell, an image to put Monmouth near the top in policy sales…up there with the giants."

Myron leaned forward on his desk. "Go on," he said.

"I've seen this spokesperson, the one that captures the right image. She can do the job. And she can probably be signed."

"She? Who is it?" Myron flailed his hands excitedly. Millard walked to the door of the office and paused:

"Linda," he said.

"Who?"

"Linda Lovelace. She's your girl from the porno movie. She's the woman for Monmouth. Her spots on TV will be real nutcrackers, Myron, real nutcrackers. She's the true image of this company. A prostitute nutcracker that gobbles down everything it can fold its lips around. Yes. We could have Linda riding a turkey with Monmouth's logo on it. And they both could be saying, 'Gobble-gobble-gobble…gobble-gobble-gobble.' Can't you see it, Myron? Linda on a turkey? The Monmouth logo? 'Gobble-gobble-gobble?' It's perfect. It's the perfect image for you and for this company."

With that, Millard left.

Millard stopped the elevator at the floor of his old office. He got off and walked the familiar path, a path he'd trod most of his working life. In contrast to his last visit, nobody stared. In fact, nobody seemed to notice him at all. When Millard arrived at his old office, he saw his name had been scraped off the door. Millard turned the knob and walked in. Jane sat at her typewriter clacking away. It was a warm sound to Millard, one that gave him a sharp twinge of nostalgia.

-This is gone, he told himself. I can't go back. Thomas Wolfe was right.

Jane turned from her work, looked up and smiled.

"Millard!" she exclaimed. "I mean Mr. Fillmore!"

"It's Millard," Millard said. He sat in one of the chairs.

"I'm so glad to see you," Jane said. She beamed.

"Glad to see you," Millard said. They stared at each other. To Millard, Jane also seemed hurt. "Real glad," Millard said. He paused.

"You're looking well," Jane said.

"Yeah. Fine," Millard said. "I came to tell you they're cashing me out. I'm on the way to accounting."

"Yes," Jane said, "I saw it coming."

"Oh?"

"The day after you left, Mr. Edgar moved into the office. I don't think they ever planned to take you back."

Millard sighed. "I know. I had to ask just to be sure. Mr. Edgar!"

"Yes," Jane said. She dropped her eyes and held her hands together in her lap.

"That toad?" Millard fumed.

"Yes," Jane said.

-The dirty frog, Millard thought, he'll run her buns off at the Zimpfer file.

Jane looked up. "I thought you'd like to know," she said brightly, "I've changed the filing system."

"Oh?"

"Yes, there's plenty of room so I just use the top two files of each cabinet," she said.

"And The Claude Zimpfer File?"

"Is no more," Jane said. "I took it home."

Millard laughed; Jane laughed.

"Frustrates the hell out of him," Jane said.

"Good," Millard said. He was pleased.

-Maybe this was what I really came back to discover, he thought.

"My show biz career is over," Millard said. "The original 'problem'...ah...it's been cured."

"Oh? What now?"

"Don't know," Millard said. "Thought at first I'd come back here. Boy, that was dumb." Jane stared at Millard and a warm light burned behind her eyes. "I thought you might call," she said softly. "I waited for you to call."

"You did?"

"Yes."

"I was too busy even to think," Millard said.

"You aren't now," Jane said.

"Well, then, maybe I will," Millard said, "if the invitation still holds."

"You know it does," Jane said. She relaxed and smiled. Millard sat back and returned the smile. Inwardly, he was happy.

At that point, Mr. Edgar came through the outer door. He looked first at Jane and then at Millard.

"May I help you?" Mr. Edgar asked.

"Hey, it's me," Millard said.

Mr. Edgar stepped back and stared. "Millard Fillmore," he said and he squinted. He looked uncomfortable.

"Yes. Sure," Millard said.

"Do you have an appointment?" Mr. Edgar asked.

Millard's face flushed in anger. "No," Millard said. He paused. "I was just leaving."

"All right," Mr. Edgar said, "I couldn't see you anyway." And with that he walked into the inner office and shut the door.

Jane grimaced and ground her teeth.

"He didn't have to do that," she hissed.

"It's OK," Millard said. "The toad and I were never close." He walked over and kissed Jane full on the lips. "I'm going to call," he said. It was his first extra marital kiss.

"Good," Jane said. "Make it soon."

Millard left and as he did so Jane's face flickered in the lights from her console that were going crazy from the irritated punches and muffled squawks of Mr. Edgar.

# Viagro 7

-Unfinished business at home can't wait, not any more, Millard thought.

Millard hiked to Grand Central and bought a ticket for his commuter. He had to wait longer than he wished and was surprised how little service was available during non rush hours. To kill time, he walked around the station. A couple of shopping-bag ladies glowered at him and one, more vexed than normal at his approach, turned her back on him and farted. It was a magnificent fart that echoed in the stone cavern, the kind young men in college produce when filled with beer and garlic and display with great pride. Millard stepped out of the field of fire but his escape was thwarted by a second bag lady that, lacking the inner resources of the first, simply waved the finger at him and cursed.

-Talent in the world is so unevenly distributed, Millard mused.

He walked to the rest room and the graffiti over the urinal told him of exotic sexual practices available in stall three. The requirement was simple; all he had to do was "show hard."

-Not any more, Millard talked back to the graffiti.

He noticed stall three was empty anyway…not that he was shopping…at least there were no feet showing underneath the door.

-The graffiti in this establishment is not current, he thought, and wondered if the management had ever heard that as a complaint.

-More than likely, he determined.

He pictured in his mind a contingent of frustrated perverts and thrill seekers marching at the front of Grand Central Station bearing signs and shouting, "Management unfair! Graffiti is not kept current." While Millard was indulging this fantasy, the door on stall three burst open and a man out of Central Casting as Scuzzo Dirtbag leered at him.

"Gotta match?" he asked. His pants were unzipped and his belt was unbuckled. Millard felt out of place in his Brooks suit…and more: he felt a target.

"No," Millard said and got the hell out.

-Sumbitch probably stood on the toilet seat to case me, Millard thought. Nothing's what it seems.

Millard arrived home around one thirty in the afternoon. He figured it'd be a good time because the kids would be in school and weren't due back for at least two hours. He and Ethel would have time to talk. Millard earlier dismissed calling as he feared starting another long distance verbal war. But now that he had arrived he regretted the decision. What if she were out?

-No matter, he concluded. I still have the keys. A man's got a right to be in his own house.

Still, he was vaguely uneasy and felt like an intruder. Lately, he'd fallen out of the habit of "going" home. Home for him had moved inside. It was this place, yes, in memory, but the center had moved; it was now in him.

Millard walked up to the front porch and tried the door. It was locked. He took out his keys to pick the one that fit. As he turned to riffle the keys, he noticed a car parked out front. It was familiar but he couldn't quite place it. He did wonder why the door was locked, however, but he assumed Ethel had gone to the store or the hairdresser's. Millard let himself into the house. He stood quietly in the hall and listened. At first he heard nothing and was even more disappointed about not calling. Then he heard a rustle and a moan. He was startled, then afraid. There was another rustle and another moan. Suddenly, it clicked for Millard: the car parked outside was a maroon MG; Steve Firth drove a maroon MG. Steve was one of the neighbors, a social acquaintance and a lawyer.

-Perhaps Ethel had retained him, he thought. It'd be natural; she already knew him and his wife, Wanda.

Another moan, another rustle, and a distinctly male sigh.

-Aha! Millard thought.

He flushed crimson in anger and started to bolt up the stairs. Then he restrained himself.

-I'll check it out, he thought and subdued his rage.

Millard walked upstairs to the master bedroom. The sounds grew louder, more frenzied and the rustlings more hurried. Millard opened the bedroom door quietly and looked through the crack. A pitcher of martinis was on the bedside stand. There were two glasses. Ethel lay back on the bed with legs splayed. Steve Firth knelt between her legs and punched her regularly and rhythmically. Ethel's heels splat randomly on Steve's upper buttocks. Squish sounds filled the room.

Millard was on the verge of bursting through the doorway and homicidally attacking Steve in a fit of despair and anger when the bathroom door opened. Wanda Firth stepped out. She was clothed only in the martini glass that she held daintily in her hand. She looked approvingly at Steve and Ethel.

-What the hell is this? Millard asked himself.

"How's it going?" Wanda asked Steve. Steve looked up.

"Fine, honey," Steve said. He smiled. Wanda smiled back. Steve looked down at Ethel.

"How are you doing?" he asked.

"Oh, just fine," Ethel said, "you are a real good pumper."

Wanda sidled up and stood beside.

"Could you refresh my drink, honey?" she asked Steve.

"Why, sure," Steve said. He kept pumping Ethel and reached over to the bedside table and picked up one of the bottles and deftly filled

Wanda's glass. Millard saw he never missed a stroke. Wanda took the glass and drank and then lay down on the bed. Meanwhile. Ethel scooted her elbows underneath her torso and sat up slightly. Her legs spread even wider and the new angle caused her generous breasts to ripple and bounce during each stroke by Steve.

-I don't believe this, Millard told himself. He had to grip the door to steady himself. They're just all just so nonchalant as hell.

Steve tucked a pillow behind Ethel's upper back. This enabled Ethel to free one of her arms and elbows so she could pick up her martini and drink more easily. Ethel sipped her drink while the pumping continued at an easy pace and her breasts quivered and jostled with each stroke that she tended to ignore because she was busy sipping. Wanda sat on the bed beside Ethel and then cupped Ethel's right breast in her hand and fondled the nipple. All three sipped martinis and other than slurps of alcohol the only sound in the room was the steady squish of Steve's penis moving in and out of Ethel.

Millard closed the door in shock and disbelief and rushed down to his den. This was not quite the homecoming he expected and it certainly precluded an easy reconciliation.

-This is crazy, Millard said as he sat down and held his head in his hands, pure crazy. He was beside himself. Oh, he'd heard of suburban swinging and wife swapping but it wasn't something that touched him personally, at least not until now. Then Millard's wild and warring emotions diminished and his mind collected itself into actual thinking. It took some effort to accomplish this, but he did it.

-Look, he told himself, you've been away; there's been terrible phone fights in which the word divorce was shouted by both parties; there was all the publicity, many pictures of myself with beautiful women; there were the rumors of my wild sex life; what can I expect? Millard twisted in his chair.

-But this? From my wife?

His gaze wandered around the room. He spied his shotgun on the wall and he knew where he stored the ammo and knew he had to shoot something. Then he saw the camera, a really classy Minolta 35 with flash he'd had a lot of fun with on vacations. He decided he had every right to shoot his wife and anybody, or even all persons with her, so he picked up the camera to record his present anguish and hoped the pictures might cut his losses in the upcoming divorce. The shotgun he dismissed as much too loud and most probably too messy. There are limits to which a man will go when discovering a flagrant wife pork and loudly creating a mess is two of them.

-It isn't too honorable snapping pictures, he admitted, but what the hell, neither is what is going on upstairs very honorable either.

Millard got up and took the camera from the shelf. He checked it out; there was plenty of film, almost a full roll. He set the camera for natural light and turned off the flash and motor drive. Then he walked quietly upstairs and cracked the door. Apparently, Ethel, Steve and Wanda had been warming up and he'd now arrived in time for the heavy action.

Millard trembled and sighed and fought back tears. But he went ahead with it. The first picture was that of Ethel laying flat on the bed with her right hand, the two middle fingers to be exact, working up and into Wanda's puddenda. Wanda stood to Ethel's right at the side of the bed. Steve still knelt between Ethel's legs and pumped. Millard realized he'd only photographed Ethel's left profile but a significant part of that was obscured by pillow. So he waited until he caught Ethel's face full and clear which he did when she groaned and jerked forward. Shot Two.

Shot Three caught Wanda straddling Ethel's head with Steve's position relatively unchanged. From where Millard shot, all he got of Ethel was the bottom of her chin and her tongue flicking in and out of Wanda's bush. Millard didn't duplicate Shot Three because he knew he couldn't get Ethel's face and he didn't figure it was worth it, at least not in court, although Wanda's expressions, especially when her eyes crossed and she yip-yip-yipped was tempting. He saw Wanda's under chin was not particularly photogenic.

Shot Four was a sure legal winner because Steve moved up and straddled Ethel over the breasts while Ethel agreeably blew his horn. Since Steve only used his far hand to rock and pump the back of Ethel's head, Millard got a good shot of Ethel's profile which was only mildly distorted from bulging cheeks. In Shot Five, as Ethel turned her head aside from a vigorous and penetrating thrust by Steve accompanied by a sharp rock and pump, Millard got a three quarter facial view. Shots Four and Five also were enhanced by switching the focus to a wider field wherein Millard caught Wanda's head buried all slurpy in Ethel's muff. Again, Wanda's neck was not photogenic.

Shot Six showed Ethel's and Wanda's face off on either side of Steve's penis. They licked and laughed and sucked and kissed and giggled and twanged. The shot was exceptional for identification so Millard clicked off Seven, Eight and Nine in rapid succession.

Shot Ten showed Ethel chomping Wanda's breasts while Steve took a break to sip his martini. Shot Eleven revealed Wanda munching Ethel's boobs while Steve finished his martini.

Shot Twelve seemed academic to Millard after One through Eleven but Millard had the film and shot it anyway. Steve packed himself into Wanda's rectum while Ethel lay back on the pillows to receive Wanda's face. Because of Steve's vigor, Wanda didn't make steady or penetrating contact with Ethel either lip or tongue-wise so Ethel helped with her index finger on her own clit, swirling and rubbing it and rolling her eyes up in her head. This was worthy, of course, for hard core porn promotions and Millard was pleased to have made at least one commercial shot.

But Millard was tired. The surge of emotions of anger, rage, hurt, shock and disbelief exhausted him. He couldn't maintain the professional photographer pose any longer. So he returned to the pain and remained amazed his sweet, or formerly sweet, Ethel was at the center of all this. Where had he gone wrong? he asked. What had he done or not done? Was Ethel that angry and hurt and frustrated? Had she changed so radically from the sweet simple girl he married? Had his notoriety caused her to fight fiction with fact? What?

Millard clicked Shot Thirteen halfheartedly. Steve blew himself away in Wanda's parallel passage and retired to the martini pitcher. Ethel and Wanda shifted to engage in a lazy little sixty nine while Steve sat on the side of the bed sweating and puffing.

Millard wanted it to be over, all of it. He set the flash for "on" and reset the focus and turned on the motor drive. He burst into the room clicking and flashing madly. The women looked up chins a-drip and stared dumbly while flashes seared their retinas. Steve didn't move; he was too pooped and too surprised. Millard waited for the multiple blue dots in their eyes to stop swimming in the air and then calmly asked Steve, "Counselor, will you be handling this divorce?"

Steve clinked his glass with his fingernail.

"I think so," he said.

Ethel buried her head in a pillow and cried. Wanda's face burned with surprise and anger.

"Well," Millard said as he tapped the camera, "remember all the evidence when you start drafting demands."

"Ah…I will; I will," Steve said.

Millard walked over to the pillow under which Ethel was hiding. He lifted it.

"I wanted to talk," he said, "but I guess this says it all."

"You…you…you lackluster prick!" Ethel sputtered.

"Yeah," Millard said, "the story of my life."

"It's all your fault," Ethel shouted. "The whole world knows you as a sex maniac."

"Sure," Millard said, "and it don't rain in Indianapolis in the summer time." He stripped the film from the camera, threw the empty camera down on the bed, and left. Steve went on drinking martinis. He was glad it wasn't a shotgun that did the shooting. Wanda called after him: "Oh, Millard? It still isn't too late to join the party."

"A no-good lackluster bastard," Ethel screamed, "that's what you are!"

Millard walked out the front door and kicked it shut. When he walked to the train station, he was in a near total funk, happy only in remembering he had the presence of mind to let the air out of all four of those little MG tires.

That evening, back in the city, Millard found himself at Jane's front door. He carried the roll of film in his hand, as he had from the time he left his former home, refusing to pitch it away from him and also refusing to pocket it and thus possess it.

Jane looked out the peephole of the door and when she recognized Millard there was the click of three locks and the growl of two chains before the door swung open.

"Hi," Jane said, "and welcome."

Millard stepped inside and Jane redid the door. It took a little while. Millard walked into the apartment and sat down, looking neither left or right. Jane followed and sat near him.

"You OK?" she asked. Millard looked down at the roll of film in his hand. "What's that?" she asked. Millard laid the film on the table.

"I took some pictures," Millard said. He then told Jane the whole story, complete with a frame-by-frame description of each picture on the roll. "I feel bad," Millard confessed, "betrayed and angry and hurt and ashamed of how I handled things."

"There, there," Jane cooed, "it's all right." She paused. "If you look at it from her angle, it's…ah…well…at least understandable."

Millard raised his eyebrows. "How?" he asked, "and I'm trying to understand. We had nothing but hard words for each other ever since I went to the doctor and took one damn blue pill and then had to leave home. From there on, it got worse. We had terrible phone fights."

"Look," Jane said, "she felt abandoned, disgraced, angry, betrayed and not a little embarrassed. Wow, and I bet her self esteem was way down to zero. And these Firth people, they were around, and obviously into swinging, and they introduced her. Simple." Jane sat back and stared into space. "I'll bet she found swinging a medium to express anger, rage, her love/hate for you and for herself."

Millard sighed. "Sure," he said, "that's good as an explanation as any for armchair psychiatry but there were other options and I think what she did was out of character, at least for her."

Jane shrugged. "Who knows?" she said. "Lust can reside massively in the most meek of individuals." And she raised her eyebrows ominously.

It's…just…just…," Millard said.

"What?"

"It's just that I can't believe I misjudged her all these years."

"Misjudged?"

"Yes. She was an Ohio girl. Can you believe that? An Ohio girl? Our sex life was good, not wild, but good. And here I catch her in one horrendous California scene. It's bizarre she changed so much and so fast."

Jane sniffed. "She had provocation, motive and opportunity…all the elements. Maybe she just seized on them and put them together. You don't know her secrets. So how does anyone get in a scene like that? There must be as many reasons as people and probably at least one more." Jane smiled. "I'm sure at heart Ethel's the same person she always was. She was…ah…well…"

"What?"

"Pushed to the limit. Strung out too far and in extremis."

Millard looked down at the floor. "I did it," he said. "She even said I did it."

"Oh hell no," Jane said, "she did it herself. You precipitated it; I'll buy that: you and your troubles and your leaving and all the ballyhoo. But basically, it was her choice. She did it to herself, Millard. Know that."

Millard lay back on the couch. He was exhausted. Soon, he fell asleep and Jane loosened his clothes and threw a blanket over him. Millard slept and dreamed troubled dreams.

In the morning, Millard awoke to the smell of frying bacon. He stumbled to the bathroom and splashed water on his face. Then he inspected himself in the mirror.

"Arghh!" he said to his reflection.

Millard straightened himself up as best he could, left the bathroom and walked to the kitchen. Jane was dressed in a soft, shimmering, pink nightgown. It was cut low and frilly around her cleavage.

Millard waved and Jane smiled back. Millard sat down at the table and Jane scurried about preparing the meal. At one point, she bent over to get a pan from under a cabinet and Millard thought of The Claude Zimpfer File and the hours and years of pleasure that simple motion by Jane had given him.

"Do it again," Millard said.

"What?" Jane asked.

"I want to see The Claude Zimpfer file."

Jane's eyes softened and she smiled slowly. Then she bent over again and waved her buns in the air. Millard walked from his chair and stood behind Jane. He cupped each buttock in a hand and rubbed and stroked and caressed.

"God, I've wanted to do that ever since I can remember," Millard said.

Jane turned around. "I've wanted you to do that ever since I can remember," she said.

Jane raised herself and placed her upper body on the top of the cabinet. She faced the wall and leaned on her elbows. Millard squeezed and kneaded Jane's buttocks and Jane relaxed and purred and looked over her shoulder. She cooed and smiled and wriggled. Millard found himself aroused. He lifted Jane's nightgown up and over her fanny and it bunched lightly up on her lower back, held there by the upward sweep of her gluteus. The bare buttocks shimmered and shivered for Millard and in the center ringlets of black hair and pink skin formed an impish vertical smile.

"The bacon," Jane said.

"What?" Millard asked.

"The bacon. We're burning the bacon," Jane said.

"Don't move," Millard said.

"All right," Jane said.

Millard walked over to the stove and turned off the burner. Then he walked back to Jane and stood behind her. He undid his trousers and let them fall to the floor. He dropped his underpants. Viagro waved in the air and a little transparent pearl of liquid gleamed at the tip. Jane's tail waved in front of Viagro and Millard could see the reddening of the skin that he'd kneaded and fondled. Millard rubbed Viagro over Jane's reddened skin. The pearl dissolved in the sheer mass of her. Then Millard centered his activity and brushed Viagro up and down the vertical smile. Jane arched herself and scooted her upper body forward on the cabinet. The motion sprouted the ringlets of hair into tendrils and the slit of pink widened. The motion also sent an array of spice bottles crashing behind the cabinet. Millard hesitated.

"Don't stop," Jane said. She arched her back even more and spread her stance slightly. Millard felt the tip of Viagro touching a warm, soft and very wet place. He eased Viagro into Jane and as he pushed inside it seemed Jane reached from inside to pull him in and welcome him. When he was buried in her, Millard stopped to enjoy his sensations. Viagro felt huge and swollen and surrounded by a juicy overcoat; there was a tingling beginning at the tip that radiated throughout his body. Millard's eyes glazed. Then, slowly, Millard slished out and in, then out and in, o-u-t and in, out and i-n, o—u—t and i—n and out-and-in and out-and-in, and outandinandoutandin and outandinandOUTandINandINandINININININ—IN and ooooOOOH!! Millard and Jane screamed together and the rest of the cooking aids on the cabinet crashed to the floor and the cabinet itself banged against the wall. Jane lay full on the cabinet and batted her arms on the surface like some crippled bird and Millard's eyes rolled up into his head and, for a moment, he lost consciousness.

As sense returned, Millard stayed inside Jane and worked himself in and out slowly. His head moved forward, then down. Jane's arms, which for a moment had become wings, retreated and snuggled up to her sides.

They stayed together for a long time and the only motion between them was the retreat and wilting of Viagro.

"God, that was great," Millard said.

"Yes," Jane said.

"Better than all the years of fantasy," Millard said.

"Much, much, much better," Jane agreed.

"You know," Millard said, "I like it that our first coupling is in this position."

Jane laughed. "Me too." She laughed again." I wouldn't have it any other way."

Millard laughed. "God bless you, Claude Zimpfer, wherever you are and whomsoever you might have been," Millard said.

"Amen," Jane said.

Millard withdrew from Jane at the point when Viagro threatened to slide out and drop. He pulled up his underpants, his pants, buttoned up and zipped, and sat. Jane scooted up on the cabinet and, as she did so, she dropped the high angle of her rump and the thin sleek nightgown fell effortlessly to her ankles. She tossed her head back and leaned forward to check the space between cabinet and wall. When she spied the wreckage of condiment bottles and wooden spoons and spices, she laughed.

"Love takes its toll," she said.

"Yeah," Millard said, "it sure does." Millard thought of Ethel and what the publicity about him helped cause. "So does the threat of love," he added.

"What?" Jane asked.

"The threat of love," Millard said. "It also takes its toll."

Jane looked puzzled. "I guess," she said. But her good mood was not to be dampened. She walked over to the stove and turned on the flame underneath the bacon. She hummed. "I've got to hurry," Jane said, "or I'll be late to work." She looked at Millard. "Mr. Edgar isn't as nice a boss as the one I used to have."

"I'm glad," Millard said.

"Besides," Jane said, "if I'm five minutes late, he tries to rearrange the files."

"Oh?"

"He tries to put the XYZ drawers near the bottom." Jane giggled and turned the bacon.

"Can't imagine why," Millard said.

"Me neither," Jane said. She cocked her head and looked up at the ceiling. "But I seem to recall another boss who did that…I forget his name."

"Hah!" Millard said as he jumped up and hugged Jane around the waist. She nestled the back of her head on Millard's shoulder. "You better not forget his name."

"It was Rhett or something," Jane said.

"Rhett?"

"Rhett Butler from *Gone With the Wind*, or Jimmy Damn Dean or some Launcelot type guy in shining armor and one hell of a lance."

"C'mon," Millard said, "he was just another gray-suited, ill-tempered executive. A real lackluster."

Jane turned around. "Not to me," she said.

Millard flushed in embarrassment and sat down. Jane turned her attention to her cooking and soon Millard was faced with bacon and eggs.

"Why don't you stay here?" Jane suggested. "At least for a while. I'll leave you a set of keys."

Millard frowned. "I don't want to impose," he said.

"Impose, hell," Jane said.

"OK, thanks," Millard said.

He smiled. Jane wolfed down her breakfast. Then she got up and walked over to Millard, hiked her nightgown and straddled him and sat down on his lap. They were face to face except Millard's head was more in line with Jane's chest. Jane kissed Millard on the forehead. She drew back and dropped the straps of her nightgown. Both breasts popped up and out and forward and Millard found his face buried between them. Jane looked up and cupped the outsides of her breasts with her hands. She slid the insides of her cleavage up and down the sides of Millard's face, over and over and over.

"Migawd," she said, "I'll be going to work with beard burn on my boobs." She leaned back and laughed.

"Good idea," Millard said. "I'd like to give you more. In fact, I'd like to send you to Mr. Edgar with beard burn all over your body...a sort of total facial Rolfing." He leaned forward and kissed the inside of each breast. Jane jumped up and back and giggled.

"That's just a reminder of what's in store for tonight," she said. "I have a bundle of face to face fantasies about you I think we ought to explore."

"Wonderful," Millard said.

Jane disappeared and Millard dawdled with his coffee. When Jane reappeared, she was ready for work. She put some keys on the table.

"Have to run," she said, "I'll be home by six."

"OK," Millard said. He arose; they shared a long, wet kiss and she was gone.

Millard sat for a while to let his breakfast digest. He felt his cheeks and was surprised at how rough his beard really was. He got up to shave and recalled his equipment was at the "Y." He puzzled about the problem and decided to return to the "Y" so he could shave and shower and change clothes.

Once at the "Y," Millard paid his rent for a week. He wanted to stay with Jane but he also wanted a place of his own, a retreat to which he could retire if things didn't work out...or if he just wanted to rest and be alone.

Millard still felt sexually excited...not in the way when Viagro nagged him, but mentally. He sensed in himself a confidence, a sureness he'd never experienced before. He thought himself sexually adept. And more. He felt himself as desirable.

-I'm proficient, he told himself. I'm damn proficient...and ready, damn ready.

Millard left the "Y" still in a state of excitement. He thought of himself as unable to fail, that all he had to do to fulfill a wild sexual destiny was to present himself.

Millard walked to Dr. Wank's office. There he confronted Dr. Wank's young, blonde and buxom nurse, one of the early women after whom he lusted when his "condition" was in full flower.

"Hi," he said, "remember me?"

The nurse looked at him carefully. She shuffled the papers on her desk.

"You one of Dr. Wank's patients?" she asked.

"Yes," Millard said, "I'm Millard Fillmore. I was here a few weeks ago. I've been with Dr. Wank a long time." Millard sat down. He read the nurse's name tag that adorned a melon size left breast. It said, "Linda Starger."

"I remember you, Linda," he said. "I am the Millard Fillmore," he boasted.

Linda looked puzzled and Millard watched her riffle through a mental file. It was here Millard learned about fame. It is as fleeting as a shooting star and once out of sight is forever out of mind. All the publicity was now lost and he was some footnote in archive and no longer in the public memory or imagination. He puzzled about this.

"Mil-lard Fill-more," she said softly. "Yes, I remember. We have your chart." She brightened up. "Did you wish to make an appointment?"

"In a manner of speaking," Millard said. He felt bold and powerful and in control. But he also mourned the loss of notoriety.

"Is it an emergency?" Linda asked.

"In a manner of speaking," Millard said. He sat back and sighed.

"What then?" Linda asked. She pouted.

Millard leaned forward in his chair and stared into Linda's eyes.

"I was here some weeks ago," Millard said, "and you came into the room while I was with the doctor. It was only for a minute." Millard bored his gaze even more deeply into Linda.

"And I was struck by your incredible beauty, grace and charm."

"C'mon," Linda said, "you want an appointment or not?"

Millard sat back in his chair and again sighed.

"Yes," he said, "I want and need an appointment and it is sort of an emergency. Only the appointment I want is with you, Linda. For openers, I'd like to take you to lunch. I meant what I said."

Linda Starger stiffened her back. "Dr. Wank doesn't like his nurses to fraternize with patients. He's very strict about that. And I agree with him. It's a good rule."

"Linda, Linda," Millard pleaded, "what I'm saying here is that I've seen you once in my life and that glimpse rattled me for weeks."

Linda softened but not much. She looked at her watch.

"What's to hurt?" Millard asked. "A nice lunch? Some pleasant conversation? From a man who's smit?"

"Who's what?"

"Smit."

"If you had a case of that, I'm sure I'd have remembered it," Linda said. "I type out progress notes."

Millard smiled and was about to give up. Then Linda laughed.

"Well-l-l-l," she hesitated.

"Fine," Millard said, "when can you leave?"

Linda again looked at her watch. "Now's good," she said. "I lunch early."

Millard arose. "Perfect," he said. "Let's go."

Linda smiled. She buzzed Dr. Wank on the intercom and told him she was going to lunch. Then she donned her coat and she and Millard walked out together. Millard asked himself what the hell was he doing and marveled at his boldness that came from nowhere. He had a near perfect situation already, what was he doing to it? And what was he doing now? He was baffled, yet he couldn't stop.

Millard took Linda to Regine's where he treated her to caviar and eggs. All through the meal, Millard talked smoothly. He elicited Jane's life story and enough of her likes and dislikes to show himself in a favorable light.

-What am I doing? Millard asked himself. I've never done anything like this before.

Still, he kept on and everything he did seemed right; nothing he did seemed wrong. By the end of the meal, he freely held Linda's hands. When they left the restaurant, she took his arm. As they walked along Central Park South, she burrowed her breast into his upper arm.

"I feel as if I've known you all my life," Linda said.

"And I, you," Millard replied, embarrassed at this hokey B film dialogue, yet convinced it was appropriate which it was. Millard stopped in the middle of the sidewalk. Linda's face glowed. Millard kissed her full on the lips and explored the inside of her mouth with his tongue. "Linda, Linda, we have this spell around us, this aura," Millard announced, "can't you feel it?"

"Oh, yes, yes!" Linda said, swept away by the silver tongue inside her head.

"Let's not wait; let's live it; let's go for it; let's check in a hotel and come together; it is so right, so right," Millard said.

"Yes, oh, yes," Linda said.

And Millard glided Linda effortlessly into the Hotel Navarro where they asked for a room. The desk clerk was not impressed.

"No luggage, no room," he said.

Millard whisked Linda to the San Moritz. There was less gliding and a tad more steering in this little journey.

"You still haven't paid your first bill, Mr. Fillmore," they told him.

They marched to the Hotel Mayflower. Here there was no gliding, little steering and a lot of tromping. The mood was fading.

"Full up," they said.

Millard got frustrated and Linda, after all the walking and the rude rebuffs at hotel counters, suffered a severe and total slip of aura.

"Look," she said, "it's getting late and I've got to get back to work. Dr. Wank is a real bear about punctuality."

"Oh, Linda, Linda," Millard tried.

"Don't Linda me," she snapped. No question about it; the aura had tanked somewhere near Columbus Circle. Whoosh and down the tubes. Linda surged ahead and walked briskly past Columbus Circle to the office. Millard followed, caught up and held her hand. They entered the medical building and rang for the elevator.

"Sorry it didn't work out," Millard said.

"You don't need to take me back to the office," Linda said, "in fact, it might get me in trouble." She looked at Millard and again her glow fired up. Linda suffered an acute flashback of aura. "I'm sorry it didn't work out either," she said. Her eyes were soft.

"I'll just ride up with you," Millard said.

"OK," Linda said.

The elevator doors opened and a group of people disembarked. Millard and Linda got on. As it happened, they were the only people going up. The door closed and the elevator started. Millard punched the stop button. He grabbed Linda and kissed her passionately.

"Here!" he exclaimed, "we've found our love nest here! It's private! It's ours!"

Linda struggled but answered Millard's tongue with her own. Her breath quickened and her aura jumped up and wreathed her head. Millard cupped her breasts with his hands. Then he moved his right hand to Linda's crotch and he rubbed furiously. Her white panty hose obstructed him so he could only rub. Probing was out of the question.

"Oh," Linda moaned from out her pulsing aura, "this is so freaky and far out. I'm really turned on!"

The elevator jumped up a foot and Millard lunged for the stop button. As soon as he hit it, the elevator stopped again. Linda wrestled free from Millard's hug and threw her skirt up over her hips. She bent over and pulled down her pantyhose which was followed in quick measure by her panties slipping down to her ankles. She lay the side of her head and hands on the waist-high wooden arm rest thoughtfully provided by the management. Millard unzipped himself and inserted Viagro.

"Oh, oh, oh," Linda moaned, "this is unreal...so kinky...so far out."

"Yes! Yes!" Millard said as he stroked powerfully and rhythmically. Linda couldn't spread her legs much because her panty hose and panties hobbled her at the knees. "Yes...ah...yes...ah...yes!" Millard called as he sloshed in and out.

"More, more more!" Linda called out, "faster, faster, faster!" she screamed.

The elevator jumped up again. Millard struggled to move Linda's bottom so he could hit the stop button. But she zagged while he zigged and he missed.

"Yes! More! Faster! Don't stop!" Linda yelled.

"Oh! Oh! Oh!" Millard yelled back.

The elevator jerked to another stop and the doors opened. Millard found himself staring into the eyes of the very short lady he'd met before in the elevator, the one who'd teased him all the way down with her shoulder blades and then slapped him and called him a pervert.

"Eeee!" Linda screamed, running off a series of orgasms like a string of firecrackers.

"Oh-h-h-h," Millard groaned as he followed not far behind her. The office crowd stood in its tracks not knowing how to proceed. Millard looked at them when he could uncross his eyes and fixed his stare on the short lady. His big moment was almost there again and Linda's was expanding from firecrackers into rockets and flares.

"Eeeeeeeeee!" Linda screamed again as she turned and swatted her own rump in paroxysms of joy. Her aura flashed like Las Vegas neon.

"Good afternoon," Millard said to the short lady. Her jaw dropped in amazement. "And a nice day, isn't it?" Millard continued. But he could no longer hold back. "Whoa ... wow-ow-ow-ow-ow!" he yelled.

The small lady clamped her jaw shut and glared. The other office workers gawked in disbelief, although some of the men smiled. The doors groaned and then snapped shut. Millard withdrew from Linda and rezipped his pants. Linda struggled but stood up quickly and pulled her panties and her panty hose up. Her hair was askew and her face flushed and her uniform severely wrinkled.

"So-o-o kinky!" she murmured. The doors opened again. Linda darted out. "Call me, Millard," she said, "and soon." She ran down the hall.

Millard waved at Linda's retreating buns and felt a silly smile spread across his face. What the hell had he done? And why? The elevator reversed direction and again opened at the floor of waiting office people. Millard stood in the rear right of the elevator, a fixed smile upon his face. He stood quiet and subdued and looked up in the air as if none of the preceeding had ever happened. He felt weak, of course, and supported himself by the handrail. The office workers quietly crowded in and the short, dark-haired woman walked up and faced Millard and frowned and turned her back. Nobody talked. This was, after all, New York. And as before, the woman leaned into Millard as the crowd pushed her back. And also as before, she nestled up to Millard and bobbed up and down and brushed side to side. She slipped her hands behind her and dug her fingers into Millard's fly. Millard had no energy for evasion. The woman fiddled with his zipper. At the next floor, the workers got off. This time, the short, dark-haired lady also got off but did not turn around. The crowd walked briskly away. When the doors closed, Millard noticed a piece of paper stuck in his fly. He grabbed it and started to toss it away but the careful fold deterred him. He opened up the paper; it said: "My name is Cynthia Block and I think I'm in love. Call 555-6121." Millard lost his grip on the hand rest and fell to the floor. When the doors opened in the lobby, Millard sat in the corner, a note in his hand and an idiot grin affixed to his face.

Millard struggled to his feet at ground floor and caught the doors before they shut and the elevator took another turn upward. He lurched through the lobby and then onto Central Park South. There he tried to regroup himself and straighten up his clothes. Millard half walked, half staggered past the Avenue of the Americas and Seventh. Once past Seventh, he felt good enough to stop and take a deep breath. He noticed he was outside the building that housed Dr. Susan Heatherton. For a moment, he thought he might visit to gather up some inner solace. But he dismissed the urge and started back for the "Y".

"Millard," a voice called.

Millard turned. It was Dr. Heatherton herself.

"Hello," he said, "I've just been thinking about you." He was glad to see her.

Dr. Heatherton smiled. "Call me Susan," she said easily. She slipped up beside Millard and took his arm. "Formality is all right in the office," she said, "but here on the street we're simply two people…people who know each other well." She flashed her teeth and Millard was dazzled. She had, he remembered well, honked his horn.

"Good. OK," Millard said, "Susan it is."

Susan looked up and down the street. She spied a hansom cab and hailed it.

"Won't you join me, Millard?" she asked. "I like to take cab rides in the park for recreation. It's sort of a coffee break."

"Uh, sure," Millard said.

The cab pulled up and screeched to a stop. Susan jumped in and Millard clambered clumsily after her.

"Tour the park," Susan commanded the driver.

"Sure, lady," the cabbie said. He clicked a watch and took off.

Susan clamped onto Millard's arm. She nestled her breasts on his elbow. She put her chin on Millard's shoulder.

"Millard, Millard," she cooed. "I've thought of you so often."

"I'm getting along just fine," Millard said. He moved away but Susan followed.

"And read about you and thought about you," Susan said. "I think of you a lot, Millard, and not as a patient…"

"I'm getting along just fine," Millard said. He shifted in his seat.

"I think of you as a man," Susan said.

"That's nice," Millard said. "I am one." He scooted to the door. Susan followed.

"Oh, Millard," Susan said as she dropped her hand into Millard's lap and squeezed his member, "I've thought of our sessions, especially the first. I measured; do you remember? I supported your penis' under side with my hand and laid the ruler on top. It was so thrilling. I think of it as the only time I ever made a penis sandwich." Susan's eyes glazed and she appeared lost in memory. All the while, she tooted Millard's member.

"I think we're near the zoo," Millard said.

"Oh, that moment is etched in memory, Millard. I'm a psychiatrist; it's true. But I'm also a woman, a woman of real flesh and blood and needful desires…"

"The zoo's right there," Millard said.

"And I found your organ perfect in every way: well-formed, straight, cylindrical, canted only slightly left but always erect…yes, always erect."

"Well, not always," Millard joked, "not these days." He laughed a brittle laugh.

Susan unzipped Millard and grabbed Viagro forcefully.

"Don't toy with me," she hissed. "This is no time for jokes."

"I'm not joking, lady," Millard said, "look, we've missed the zoo. Don't you think we ought to enjoy our ride here?"

"I am. I am," Susan said. She withdrew Millard's organ and beat it forcefully and ferociously. To Millard's surprise, it stiffened. Susan jumped astride Millard and hiked her skirts.

"Cabbie, go up by the reservoir and keep your eyes front," Susan called out.

"Whatever you say," the cabbie replied.

Millard grabbed the door handle. He tried to open it. He wanted to jump out.

"We could take a walk," Millard said, "the park's nice up here."

"Quiet," Susan said. She pulled her skirt to her waist. Millard saw a garter belt and black lace panties. He was surprised. That costume was from a different era. Susan expertly fingered the crotch of her panties over to the left side and deftly steered Millard into her vagina. Then she squatted down fast and hard, nailing Millard to the seat.

"The Planetarium," Millard said. "We could visit the Planetarium. Nothing beats an afternoon light show."

"Watch this," Susan growled, "I'm gonna roll comets through your head."

Millard fumbled with the door latch. Susan pounded her crotch down on Millard with the insistency of an air hammer. Rat-ta-ta-ta-ta-ta-ta-ta-ta! Rat-ta-ta-ta-ta-ta-ta-ta!

"Maybe a museum. You like art? We could go to Fricks."

Ta-ta-ta-ta-ta-ta-ta-ta!

Susan's eyes turned up in her head and she boxed Millard's ears with the palms of her hands. Little explosions sounded inside Millard's head and, sure enough, comets flashed.

"Or the Bird Sanctuary? Would you like to see the Bird Sanctuary?" Millard tried to protect himself around the head and shoulders. The physical assaults were dangerous. Susan grabbed Millard's hair from behind and stuffed his head between her breasts. "M-m-m-m-rf? M-m-m-m-m-rf?" Millard called. He couldn't breathe.

"Row-ah-ow! Row-ah-ow! Row-ah-ow!!" Dr. Susan Heatherton screamed.

"M-m-m-m-m-rf! M-m-m-m-m-rf!" Millard said.

"RowOW! RowOW! RowOW!" Susan called.

Then she relaxed and slumped back and Millard's head was released. He gasped for air. Susan straightened up and abruptly withdrew. She broke straddle and sat back beside Millard in one clean motion.

"That was invigorating, wasn't it?" she asked. "I love lunch time in New York. Just what the doctor ordered. So free, so spontaneous, so…now."

"We could have gone to the Wollman Rink," Millard groused. His battered organ, sawed on each side by his zipper, wilted and glowed red. Susan patted the tip and replaced Viagro in his cotton sheath and zipped him up.

"Go back to Central Park South," Susan commanded the driver.

"Sure," said the cabbie. He swung around and headed south.

Susan hummed to herself and took out a make-up kit. She repaired the damage to her face and hair and straightened her clothes. She appeared quite happy. Millard lay in the corner of the cab. He felt he didn't have the strength left to sit up.

"Hell, we could have seen the damn Frick Collection," he mumbled, "it was just across the street."

Once on Central Park South, Dr. Susan Heatherton jumped out of the cab. There was spring in her legs and she looked enervated and her motions were crisp and brisk. She paid the cabbie and left him a fifty dollar tip.

"It was great, Millard," she said, "and you were simply wonderful. Do call, please! Ta, ta!"

Susan bounced off onto Central Park South and strode to her offices swinging her pocketbook and tossing her hair back and smiling. She looked every inch a happy woman. Millard couldn't move from the corner.

"Nobody sees the Frick Collection any more," he told himself, "there's just not a whole hell of a lot of interest in it."

"Where to, Mac?" the cabbie asked.

Millard brought himself up enough to whisper Jane's address.

"These nooners are a bitch," the cabbie growled.

Millard couldn't find the strength to agree by any sound or sign but he assented as forcefully by spirit as he was able.

When Millard staggered into Jane's apartment, she was there and waiting. She was dressed in black leather with spike-heeled boots. The tips of her bra were cut out and Jane's nipples poked out pinked and erect. In one gloved hand she held a riding crop. Silver studs adorned the outfit. There was no crotch.

"I left work early," Jane explained, "and went shopping." She smiled and turned around. "You like the outfit? I told Mr. Edgar I had the flu." Millard stared and his jaw went slack. "I never asked," Jane said, "but are you interested in discipline?"

"Oh…my…gawd," Millard said as he fell back against the door and crumpled into a heap on the floor. Which, of course, Jane took as a sign of submission and gleefully set to work.

# Viagro 8

For the next two weeks, Millard wallowed in a sea of boobs and bushes. Jane was not into discipline and leather as much as costumes, much to Millard's relief. One night she was Nancy Reagan; another she was Gloria Steinem; then she was Ann Bolyn or Princess Grace or Jackie-O or Bo Derek or Bella Abzug. Later, she was Lady Macbeth, Ophelia or Madame DeFarge with knitting needles. Millard vividly remembered the knitting needles; they smarted. Then it was Constance Bennett, Marlene Dietrich, Claudette Colbert and Lizzie Borden. Then Janis Joplin and Grace Slick. The most unsuccessful character was Joan of Arc. Millard had trouble producing tongues of fire through sheet metal and mail. Burning at the stake on top of an electric range was less than spectacular.

Linda Starger continued her interest in elevators and took the act everywhere, including Bloomingdale's, Gimbel's, Macy's, The Harvard Club and the editorial offices of Time-Life.

Susan Heatherton persevered with moving objects. She grew especially fond of sunroofs. The Mercedes allowed her to stretch out on top in great comfort while Millard stood on the seat to service her. But a Volkswagen tested her mettle and resolve, slipping as she did off the rounded roof and nicking herself badly on the snout of the license plate light. After that, they moved inside…hansom cabs, subways, city buses, motorcycles (two-wheel, three-wheel and one side car), dune buggies, a Jeep, roller skates and once, without success, a gas-powered skateboard.

Cynthia Block, perhaps because she was short, developed a penchant for high places. She liked to lay back with her head upside down and over an abyss. She liked The Chrysler Building, The Empire State Building and both World Trade Towers. There were quickies at the UN and Pan Am and in the Crown of the Statue of liberty. More than one tower guard chased Millard and Cynthia and not a few times did they narrowly escape arrest. Cynthia wanted Millard to take her to Chicago. But the farthest they got was the George Washington Bridge where, for a short while, they stopped traffic.

But these were not the only ladies in Millard's life. There were waitresses, clerks, secretaries, fashion models, bored housewives from Far Rockaway, society ladies, teeny boppers, streetwalkers inexplicably working free, hotel maids, opera buffs, theater buffs, ballet buffs (one of whom surprised Millard with an unbuffered schvantz larger than his own), retired widows from Damrosch Park, coeds from Fordham University, a bassoon player from Julliard whose love for her instrument proved entertaining and instructive, a few tourists, excepting those from Idaho who were too fat. And the acme of the casual encounters, a shopping bag lady who, upon spying Millard, threw her skirt over her head and cackled an obscene and public invitation and tried to smother him in aged and vintage crinoline.

Millard was mystified. None of this sexuality appeared related to his name or his former prominence. In fact, none of the women recognized his name in relation to his former image. That was curiously forgotten. Millard thought he might have developed a scent like a pheromone, something that drove women wild and caused them to act without restraint. And Viagro cooperated by rising to each occasion. That was the most amazing part of all to Millard: Viagro never gave up. He could give up; but Viagro didn't. He could drop; he could faint; he could slump in exhaustion; but Viagro couldn't wilt if the situation was there. Millard lost a quick twenty pounds. He grew haggard and weak; flecks of gray appeared in his hair; his eyes sunk in their sockets and were rimmed black with fatigue. The ennui grew and Millard started to look for a way out.

One day, as he ran from a woman stevedore, he found himself in a phone booth. There he dialed Binky. He hoped, if nothing else, to hear a male voice, or any voice without that odd and plaintiff note of sexual suggestion.

"Hello," Binky said.

Millard was surprised he hadn't reached the answering service.

"It's me, Millard."

"Hey-y-y-y," Binky said, "where you been?"

"Around."

"I've been trying like hell to reach you."

"Oh?"

"I've got super news."

"OK, Binky, you got the financial report?"

"Oh, yes...and more."

"More?"

"Now, Millard, brace yourself. You know I tried to dissolve every thing?"

"Yes." Millard braced for the worst.

"Well, I hoped to cut our losses or let Millard Fillmore, Inc. suck up the deficits."

"And?"

"Well, all the consultants left bang! now. But Myron and Ben stayed. They had to; they were hung with huge inventories. They wanted to see if they could unload them."

"No law suit? We didn't get sued?"

"No! And the weirdest thing happened, sales picked up."

"What?"

"Sales picked up!"

"You're kidding."

"It's true. Ben and Myron even noted a surge after the last Enquirer story. Can you believe it? The book's going great…not best seller but steady…and the paraphernalia is going great…everything is great!"

"Wow," Millard said. "Why?"

"The only thing I can think is your image has penetrated the public psyche."

"What?"

"You're a trademark like the Gerber Baby. Nobody worries about the Gerber Baby being real. She's a middle-aged and fat housewife somewhere by now. But her image still sells. That's what happened to you."

"You mean…?"

"I mean the 'dignity' note we hit kicked the gong just right. It registered in the market place and vibrated in the public ear. We're set forever. Millard Fillmore is now like the Gerber Baby. He's the authority and the trusted symbol of sexual advice and paraphernalia. Hell, who needs you any more?"

Millard shuffled in the phone booth. He got flashed by a female junior executive so he turned away.

"Good. Now look," Millard said, "that's wonderful and all. I'm not going to tell you what's happening now because it's a little bizarre. But I am interested in the money. What about the money?"

Binky took a deep breath.

"Millard, we've paid everybody off. We're even current with Myron and Ben."

"Everybody?"

"Everybody…all the consultants, lawyers, PR firms, CPA's, ad men…the whole lot."

"And the money?"

"I can let you have one thousand dollars a day. That's cash. Every day. Starting back two weeks ago. And that's just your personal cut. The corporation is even fatter."

Millard staggered and fell against the phone booth. "One thousand dollars a day?!" he mumbled. A stockbroker-type lady licked the glass nearest Millard's face. He smiled and turned his back. "How can I pick it up?" Millard asked. "How do I get it?"

"I'm ready for you," Binky said. "I've got a new card that acts like a check. You also can draw cash against it. Just try to keep it under one thousand a day, OK? And I have our books ready and open. You can look at them anytime. Bring your own accountant and lawyer."

The stockbroker lady followed Millard's turn. She now licked the glass nearest Millard's crotch and gestured and pointed wildly.

"Leave the card for me at the 'Y'," Millard said. "I'll pick it up at the resident's desk."

"So that's where you've been."

"Not really," Millard said. He sighed. The stockbroker lady wrapped her arms and legs around the booth and tried to mate with it. "I've got to run now."

"Sure," Binky said, "I'll leave it at the 'Y'." He hung up.

Millard waited for a break in the lady's surging and when he found the opportunity, he burst through the doors and ran like hell to a subway entrance. Once in the subway, Millard disappeared into the crowd. He wanted out and now he was overjoyed he had the money to do it right and permanently. It was, Millard mused, almost past time. Jane was far into ugly and hurtful pain trips and was planning a dress up retrospective of archetypical hostile bag ladies with various weapons. Linda wanted to invade certain bureaucracies in Washington with the elevator act, particularly Health and Human Services, the Department of State and the U.S. Senate and, for some unknown reason, the Bureau of Indian Affairs. Susan was now talking lunch with water skis and hang-gliders and Cynthia wanted to rent a hot-air balloon.

"My time is now," Millard said aloud to himself. A lady looked up, frowned and moved away. Then she took a second look and moved closer with an odd smile on her face. Millard changed cars.

Millard rode the subway a long while, changing trains and directions frequently. He found it relaxing. Finally, he returned to the "Y" where he sat down by himself in his room and made some decisions. First, he told himself, he'd break with Jane. That was no problem; she'd already settled for an open relationship. And there wasn't much to move out because most of his belongings, what little he had, were at the "Y". Then there was Dr. Susan Heatherton. Professionally, he'd gotten what he'd paid for: an awareness of his father's attitude toward him and the effect on his life of an albatross of a name. Socially, he'd gotten more than he'd bargained for: a woman who liked to mate on moving objects. Susan he could leave. Linda Starger could be abandoned in an elevator and Cynthia Block could be left without pitons or ropes on the top of any high building.

-OK, Millard thought, so much for the steady love life.

The casual love life was not so easy to dismiss. Millard could not avoid it; it just seemed to happen. So Millard decided to do the next best thing.

-I'll walk away, Millard told himself. I'll simply walk away.

Millard lay back in the bed. He felt relieved and a little less fettered.

-What about Ethel and the kids and the divorce? he asked.

This question shattered his former feeling of security and forced him to sit up.

-I don't know, he admitted. I just don't know.

He fidgeted with the bed. Two additional questions came in a rush: the name problem and the father problem.

-I don't know about those, either, Millard thought, although back in his mind he felt some solutions stirring. He had the same feeling he used to have when he was wrestling with some of his tougher investment calls, a tickling in the back of his head that preceded a breakthrough.

"Well," Millard said to the wall, "I can find out about the Ethel situation."

Millard forced out of his mind the ugly pictures he'd recorded. He got up, left the room and traveled to the phone bank in the lobby. Enroute, he stopped at the resident's desk and asked if anything had been left for him.

"Yeah," the clerk said. He reached back to a pigeonhole and pulled out an envelope with Millard's name on it. He tossed it to Millard. Millard picked it up and walked away. At the phone bank, he opened it. It was a Master Credit Card II with his name stamped on it. Binky had written a note. It said: "Have a nice time."

Millard sighed. Between this money and what he'd taken from Monmouth he knew he didn't have to worry about finances for months. Whatever plan he made, it was already funded. Millard picked up a dog-eared and frayed directory. He looked up Steve Firth's office number and dialed. He really didn't want to talk to Steve, or Wanda for that matter, but he had to start somewhere.

"Turnbull, Finkel, Wiener and Firth," a receptionist said.

"Steve Firth," Millard said, "Millard Fillmore calling. I do not want to talk to any of your Wieners."

"One moment, puh-lease," said the voice.

There was a click.

"Steve Firth's office," said another voice. This one was younger and more lilting.

"Millard Fillmore for Steve Firth," Millard said.

"Please hold."

Millard waited. He fully expected to be told Steve was out, or in court, or in conference, or out to lunch.

"Millard? It's Steve," Steve Firth said. "Was hoping you'd call."

Millard was taken aback. The immediate contact seemed abrupt and derailed his train of thought.

"Yeah," Millard said. "Steve, this is Millard," he fumbled. Steve waited. Millard collected his thoughts. "I'm calling about the divorce."

"Right," Steve said, "I knew it was you because I answered the phone. We've decided to go for a no-fault or an uncontested. The terms are simple. Ethel wants to sell the car and house and furnishings, less whatever personal items you want, and split the profits down the middle."

"OK," Millard said.

"You sure you want to handle this?" Steve asked. "Wouldn't you be more comfortable being represented by counsel?"

"It's OK," Millard said. "I'll get one later. I just want to hear the terms."

Steve cleared his throat.

"Ethel doesn't want anything for herself. She's had her consciousness raised."

"I know," Millard said, "I took pictures at the raising."

"Yes," Steve said. He cleared his throat again. "She doesn't want support or alimony."

"Good."

"Now the kids...," Steve began.

"What about them?" Millard asked. He tensed against the phone bank.

"Ethel's sent them to private schools. She didn't feel they could continue to live at home what with your notoriety and all."

"And?"

"And she wants you to foot tuition and support up to age eighteen, which isn't far away, and then four years of college if they so choose." Millard thought about that. "I agree," he said.

"I think you ought to get a lawyer," Steve said.

"I will," Millard said, "but go ahead and draw up the papers along the lines you've stated."

"OK," Steve said.

Millard paused. "What about Ethel? Where is she? Is she all right?"

Millard heard some papers rustling.

"She wants to talk to you," Steve said. "She left a phone number."

"OK," Millard said. He fumbled in his pocket for a pen. He found it and took it out and then tore a scrap of paper from the margin of the phone book. "Go ahead," Millard said.

"The number is 586-6311," Steve said.

Millard wrote it down. "Thanks," he said. There was a pause.

"There's one other thing," Steve said.

"Yes?"

"About the photographs."

"Yes?

"Wanda and I and Ethel want them back."

"After the divorce is struck," Millard said, "you're welcome to them."

Millard heard the phone scrape Steve's chin.

"In a sense," Steve said, "we could make a case for blackmail here."

"In another sense," Millard countered, "I could go for adultery and unfit mother and custody."

"Ahem," Steve said.

"Don't push it," Millard said, "I just want a fair settlement. And so far it seems I'm getting it."

"But we want the photographs," Steve insisted.

"And you'll get them," Millard promised. "Listen," Millard said, "I think it's pretty shitty you and Wanda drawing Ethel into that. I don't care about your life style, but when it comes to my wife, or a woman soon to be my former wife, I care…or rather I did care." Millard thought about what he said. "I want to be perfectly clear about this," he added because he wasn't sure what he really did say.

"Well," Steve said, "a foursome is the recommended number. Wanda had been working on Ethel a long before you got famous. I never got around to working on you because there wasn't time. It was my fault. You should have been there."

"Working? You mean this stuff was going on all around us all the time and I never knew?"

"Yes," Steve said, "but it is just a neighborhood thing. No big deal."

Millard turned around and leaned against the ledge.

"I didn't know," Millard said.

"You do now," Steve said. "You and Ethel were the only hold outs."

"All around us?" Millard asked.

"The Bakers, The Smiths, The Provolones, The Pindorps…all of us."

"Holy shit," Millard said.

Millard was outraged and angry with himself for being so unobservant. In another way, he was jealous because Wilomina Pindorp had the nicest boobs he'd ever seen and he had had a mad desire to stuff his mouth with both of them. Now that chance was gone forever.

"So don't kick Ethel too hard," Steve said.

Millard grew angry and embarrassed. He was angry about not knowing and embarrassed now that he did. He bit back some harsh words.

"OK," Millard said, "I'll have an attorney get in touch. I'm not going to mention pictures to him. That's informal and between us."

"If we don't get them, it could become very formal," Steve said.

"Not to worry," Millard said and he hung up. "Shit!" he exclaimed as the phone rattled on the hook, "I've missed two shots at Wilomina Pindorp forever."

Millard walked up and down for a few minutes to calm himself. Then he returned to the phone and dialed the number Steve had given him.

"Hello," said a young male voice.

"I'm calling for Ethel Fillmore," Millard said.

"Sure," said the voice. The phone rattled against a hard surface. "Ethel, it's for you."

Millard waited. Next he heard the phone clink as it was picked up.

"Hello?" Ethel said.

"It's Millard," Millard said.

"Oh, Millard, how nice of you to call," Ethel said. "I take it you've talked to Steve?"

"Yes."

"And the terms are satisfactory?"

"Yes."

"Wonderful."

"Ethel, where are you?"

Millard heard Ethel take a deep breath.

"I'm in SoHo. Well, near it. I'm on Horatio Street, right off Jackson Square. This is a loft."

"A loft?"

"A loft."

"What do you do in lofts?" Millard asked.

"We make art," Ethel said.

"And the young man, is his name Art or he does he make art or is it a case of both? He doesn't sound old enough for either."

"Oh, yes," Ethel purred, "he's old enough. He's twenty three." Millard slapped his forehead with his hand. "And right now," Ethel continued, "he's making ultrasound milieus."

"What?"

"Ultrasound milieus."

"What are they?"

"Well," Ethel said, "Pieter constructs, or uses, spaces in basic unseen colors and alters them so that the projection of ultra sound in the space creates this totally invisible emanation…"

"Wait a minute," Millard said, "who's Peter?"

"Pieter. There's an 'i' in it. It's Pieter."

"Are you also the 'I' getting it on and in with Pieter?"

"That, too," Ethel said easily, "now the milieus are as small as a one-inch cube or as large as Pennsylvania. The one we're working on now is the loft itself. We're coloring it and altering it."

"How do you see an emanation that's soundless and invisible?"

"That's the art of it. You see rainbows, can't you?"

"Yes."

"Same thing."

"No," Millard said, "rainbows come from light. You can see light. Sound is different."

"Whatever," Ethel said curtly, "the milieus…"

"Wait a minute!" Millard yelled, "you said ultra sound. Nobody hears ultra sound."

"Oh, Millard," Ethel said, "you are such a Philistine. That's another part of the art of it. Of course you can't hear it. That's why we use ultra sound. How silly! You are just a silly."

Millard twisted to and fro on the phone line. He was in a state of high agitation.

"You're telling me you're living with an artist named Pieter who's twenty three…"

"We're lovers," Ethel said, "and we live together. But we're not exclusive."

"…and he's making…"

"Milieus."

"…milieus out of spaces with sounds no one can hear to produce emanations and areas in colors no one can see?"

"You've got it!" Ethel exclaimed. "I didn't think you could understand or begin to grasp it but you did! Oh, Millard, I'm so proud of you. You've taken a giant leap!"

Millard spun around and leaned on the ledge. He stared directly into the phone. The bands of chrome distorted his face.

"OK," Millard said, "thanks, I think. I have felt like leaping more than once."

"Millard, Millard," Ethel gushed, "it's so wonderful being here, being on the cutting edge of art. Cosmopolitan was right; I've wasted so many years. Did I tell you how Pieter signs his work?"

"No."

"He uses a dog whistle, one of those ultrasound little long chrome things. We've got a case of them. Isn't that clever? He tacks up a dog whistle on a milieu. Oh, Millard, the other day we were in Rockefeller Plaza and Pieter got inspired. He started walking around and sensing and meditating, he learned that with the Hare Krishnas, you know, while working airports, and he wandered up to St. Patrick's and he walked all around it, and then through it, and Millard, it was so thrilling, just to watch genius functioning, and he declared St. Patrick's a milieu! Not just a milieu…his milieu. And right then and there, since it was perfect as is, and needed no modification, no alteration, although Pieter did have a small quibble about the placement of the holy water fonts, he took out a dog whistle and a hammer and a nail and signed his work right there. He nailed his signature to the front wall by the door."

"Signed it? He signed St. Patrick's Cathedral?"

"Yes! Yes! Isn't that thrilling? Now all the world, whether they know it or not, can experience one of Pieter's most priceless milieus."

"Of course," Millard said. He decided to agree with everything. "Then what happened?"

"Well," Ethel said, "when he nailed his whistle on the wall, the police arrested him for defacing property and took him away. But he didn't mind. No, indeed, Pieter will pay any price for his art. And he told me long ago one of the qualities of the Fascist Police Pig is non-appreciation of art so an arrest was not unexpected. So I paid the fine willingly."

"Ho-kay," Millard said, "look, Ethel, I'm glad things are working out so well for you. Now how can I get in touch with the kids?"

"Oh," Ethel said, "until the divorce would you mind working through Steve on that? I've made no restrictions but I would prefer you work through him. They're in good schools. And they wanted to go; they really did. You don't know. You just can't know the ugliness you caused them at school."

"Yeah," Millard said, "I can imagine."

"I have to go now," Ethel announced, "Pieter and I are looking for a flying buttress."

"They're awful nice this time of year," Millard offered.

"…because we're sure it'll produce a really superb emanation to place in our next milieu."

"In the milieu? You can place things in a milieu?"

"In here. In the loft. This is our first together milieu and his latest. Then we're going out to check out the George Washington Bridge."

"Ethel?"

"Yes?"

"The George Washington Bridge will not fit in your loft."

"Oh, you're so silly. If you want to visit, you're welcome," Ethel said. "We don't have a mail box. Just walk west on Horatio on the north side and look for the dog whistle on the door, OK? You're welcome. As I said, we're not exclusive. We're lovers but we're not exclusive. I may have something for you for all the old times."

"Fine," Millard said, "and if I come I'll check for emanations and sounds and ask to walk over the bridge."

"Aren't you wonderful? Such spirit. You have opened your senses to the world," Ethel said.

"Yes, that's true," Millard said, "and you have led me to it. Look, I'll look for the dog whistle and open my senses up fully for the rest."

"OK," Ethel said, "as concept, it takes some getting used to but you are doing so well."

"I'm sure."

"'Bye," Ethel said.

"Good luck with the flying buttress," Millard said.

Ethel hung up. Millard rested his forehead against the cool metal of the phone and exhaled slowly and banged his head against the booth.

In the days following the conversation with Ethel, Millard tied up the loose ends of his New York life. He visited his kids and found them happy in their present situations. Also, they seemed to bear no resentment at the planned divorce. They accepted it easily…mainly, Millard thought, because over ninety percent of their peers at school also were dealing with divorced parents. There were no emotional scenes. Millard felt no great sense of loss. In a way, he always was a stranger in his own home and his attempts to "belong" had failed. He'd always felt at home at home but not that he really belonged there. He had to face it; his own kids were strangers.

On the sexual front, Millard found breaking off with Jane, Susan, Linda and Cynthia also stopped casual encounters. This fact seemed to fit Millard's pheromone theory. Inactivity stopped scent production...if that's what it was. Anyway, he was no longer harassed.

On the legal front, Millard hired an attorney he'd met at the Businessmen's Club. His name was Donald Sharp and young Donald waltzed right through the divorce preliminaries with ease. Donald and Steve Firth both recommended an out-of-state settlement that meant a western trip for Ethel and Pieter. And Pieter pinned a dog whistle on the Grand Canyon and got arrested by a ranger but other than that the trip was a success.

After the divorce, Millard returned the film to Steve and then sat down with Don to settle finances. He placed the Master Card II into Don's hands and gave him power-of-attorney over the corporation and his personal share of the monies. He also had him set up some revocable trusts and tax shelters so the Millard Fillmore, Inc. money was tucked away, yet usable. Don was overjoyed with his assignments because he was young and just getting started. Finally, Millard brought up with Don a legal matter about which he'd thought deeply.

"Don, I need to change my name," Millard said.

"Why?" Don asked.

"I've never liked Millard Fillmore...never. And with the notoriety it once had and, to an extent, still has, I want free of it."

Don Sharp's mind spun a few turns and then he smiled.

"It's not difficult," Don said. He took out a pad and pencil. "What name do you want?"

Millard sat back and thought.

"For a while, I thought Warren G. Harding had a nice ring to it," Millard said, "and then I thought of James Buchanan." Don Sharp's eyebrows raised. Millard laughed. "I also thought of Zip Flash and Sparkle Plenty and Meat."

"Sparkle Plenty?"

"…or Studs Grit and Stant Tough and Shiny Chrome Dork."

"OK, OK," Don raised his hands, "enough already. What's it going to be?"

"Ashley Benton Longerbone."

"Ashley? That's southern, Millard. You're not southern. And Longerbone? With your history? That's ridiculous."

Millard sighed. He picked up the telephone directory on Don's desk and flipped through it. He closed his eyes and riffled and riffled. Then he stabbed his index finger to a page.

"There it is," he said without looking. "That's the one."

Don leaned over and read the name.

"Guido Salvatore? You want to change your name to Guido Salvatore?"

Millard shut his eyes and riffled and stabbed again.

"Ace Car Rental?" Don asked.

Again, Millard riffled and stabbed.

"Bertha Prindle?"

Again.

"Jesus Garcia Gonzales?"

Millard repeated the process.

"Reinquist, Bartles and Park?"

Again.

"Steve Spalding?"

"Is that what it says?" Millard asked. His eyes brightened and he looked at the page.

"That's it," Don said.

"Then that's the one," Millard said. He picked up the directory and stared.

"I like it. It rings. Steve Spalding. Steve Spalding."

"OK," Don said, "if you're sure."

"I'm sure," Millard said, "but add a middle initial, will you? Not a name, just an initial. 'B' is good. Steven B. Spalding. I like it." Millard felt free and alive and relieved and expectant all at the same time.

Some weeks later, Steven B. Spalding took a job in Columbus, Ohio. One of Millard's college friends, Tad Baker, was vice president and comptroller of Mordant Life Assurance. They'd kept in touch through the years and the relationship was as much professional as personal. Tad hired Steve even after Steve told him his story.

"I always liked your work at Monmouth," Tad explained, "and my man in investments here still thinks Savings Bonds and Fannie Maes and Ginny Maes are as risky as World War II B girl fan dancers." Tad paused. "He's retiring in a few weeks. We can use you."

"Great," Steve said, "there won't be any static about my past?"

"'Course not," Tad said. "you work under me and I run my own shop. I also file and hold your job application and work history. It's private."

"Good," Steve said. He wanted to break with the past.

Steve rented a small house in Upper Arlington on Columbus' north side. He furnished it. It was exciting to start a new life under a new name although he had a lot of trouble answering to Steve. He called Don Sharp once a week and found the Millard Fillmore, Inc. bonanza was steadily fading, as expected. Yet there was a stream of money out of which he paid obligations. Don developed a deft financial touch and the trusts and shelters grew. Steve wondered to himself why he didn't take the money and go on a high-living binge. Somehow, that didn't tempt him, not after the weeks he was in the public eye and the sensuality afterward.

-No, Steve thought, a steady job, a quiet life, a smaller city and a nice woman somewhere in the future…that's all I need, all a sensible man ever really needs.

When the man he was to replace retired, Steve thought he'd arrived. They gave him a nice office and he was allowed to choose his own secretary. The job itself was easy compared to Monmouth. It was significantly smaller in dollar amount but Ohio law was tricky and unfamiliar and the politics of Mordant investments were equally as tricky. Steve could see he'd be busy.

The secretary Steve chose was a bright, young and industrious girl named Marcie Thompson. Marcie had an associate degree in business administration from Franklin University and had also graduated from a local secretarial school called Columbus Business University. Physically, she resembled Jane, a fact Steve recognized only after she was on the job. She was, however, slightly heavier in all the right places.

-Corn fed women are comfortable, Steve thought at times but not so often that it was a problem.

Marcie took off on the run from the first day. She ordered office supplies, new files, wooden desks, rugs, intercoms, phones, an IBM, judges chairs, plants and decorative knick knacks. Steve was pleased to see his office quickly bloomed all around him.

Marcie was personable and talkative and Steve found himself at ease. In all, he felt comfortable and settled and happy. Tad was an undemanding boss and dealt with the president and the board alone. That was a relief to Steve who appreciated Tad's role as buffer and flak catcher.

When the new filing cabinets arrived, Marcie placed them in Steve's office, to the front and right of his desk. She spent days setting them up and when the bustling stopped, Steve checked them over and pronounced them A-1, which they certainly were. Marcie was happy.

One day, in a fit of absent-mindedness, Steve called Marcie into his office.

"May I see The Claude Zimpfer file?" he asked. He'd really wanted something else and was surprised at his own words.

Marcie walked over to the file bank, bent over and shuffled through the Z's. Her fanny popped into the air and waved. Steve noticed it was a bit more generous than Jane's and much better rounded, if that were possible. But Steve was shocked at his own request. Moreover, he was sure there were no files in the Z's…or at least there hadn't been when he'd inspected them a few days ago. Steve also was shocked at his asking Marcie to look for a file he knew could not exist.

-Where is my mind? he asked. What the hell is happening?

Marcie's fanny jiggled and bobbed. It was quite a show. Finally, she got up and walked to Steve with a file in her hand.

"Here it is," she announced.

"What?" Steve asked.

"The Claude Zimpfer file," Marcie said. She smiled and Steve thought he detected a knowing toss of her head.

"Oh?" Steve said. He looked at the file. It said, "Claude Zimpfer." He opened it. There was nothing inside.

"It's empty," Steve said.

Marcie sat down. "Of course," she said. She crossed her legs and hiked her skirt over her knee. Suddenly it seemed that innocent motion was performed provocatively. "I made it up from your doodles."

"Doodles?"

"Yes, do you know you write that name a lot? You scribble it on scrap paper and in the margins of boring letters, on your desk pads…everywhere. I figured it had some significance so I started up an official file."

"Oh," Steve said. He was astounded. "Thanks," he said, "that's good work and very forward thinking." He paused. Why the hell was he doodling? "Would you put it back, please? You must excuse me. I suppose I was doodling aloud in my head here. I'm sorry." He forced a chuckle.

Marcie smiled. "No problem." She arose and took the file and replaced it.

-Is it my imagination? Steve asked, or are her hips swaying?

Marcie pertly bobbed her buns up and down and returned. Steve noticed her eyelids looked heavy.

"Will there be anything else?" Marcie asked. Steve noticed her voice was definitely husky.

"No," Steve said. "Thank you." He shook. Marcie left. Steve gripped the front of his desk for support. It was then he noticed he'd grown a hard-on. His eyebrows shot up in amazement.

=Hi, Viagro said.

-Migawd! Steve answered. You! You're back?!!

=None other, Viagro replied. Look, Millard…

-It's Steve!

=Whatever. Look, Steve, you and I, we're going to ravish these corn fed cuties and probably take that little Marcie to Vegas for the weekend.

-No!

=Oh, yes! It's going to happen. This will make New York look small time. You like what I did in New York, didn't you? Especially after I stopped talking? That was all me, you know. Pheromones, my ass. I got your pheromones hanging right here. You're gonna see such action you're gonna wind up hating the sight of splayed out crotches of naked ladies…

-No!

=Of course down deep you knew. You thought you were Errol Flynn, didn't you? Or Casanova? Or Don Juan? Haw! You are one lackluster man, my friend, and I cured you and now that's all a thing of the past. No matter what name you're now using. I killed lackluster in you forever. You are lackluster no more.

-No!

=Sure, Viagro said, lackluster's like virginity, when it's gone, it's gone forever. Now here's our plan…

## The End

# About the Author

Here's 44288 just weeks before Columbus State Hospital issued his number. He's chopping wood behind his mother's lovely Granville, Ohio home. Alcoholism, anxiety neurosis, and agoraphobia were a tad misunderstood in the late 1950's. Treatment was standard. It began with a visit from the Licking County Sheriff's Department. Four armed deputies arrived with holsters unsnapped. They surrounded and quickly put the afflicted in handcuffs and leg irons, tossed him in the back of a flashing, cherry-topped black and white taxi; splayed him out in back, locked him up tight, and provided perpetual armed observation. The deputies then transported this lucky person to Newark, Ohio Jail where his own personal deputy, who weighed slightly under the normal weight of a Clydesdale Horse, took him in his back seat while still chained to Columbus State Hospital. Once there, the body was turned over to another four men in white uniforms with black, clip on and tear away bow ties who were bigger than an average Big 10 college football tackle. They watched while said sufferer was weighed, fingerprinted, photographed (front and side), over an official and personal number he was awarded and could wear with pride for the rest of his natural life. His monies, personals and driver's license were all confiscated. After this, he was escorted by these same four, white-suited men and thrown into a maximum security isolation room which, in defiance of myth, was not padded, but actually a bare stoned 8x10 cell, floored with hard terrazo and walled in yellow brick blocks. The door was two inches thick and the wood was steel-sheathed with a huge peephole crudely bored right through at eye level. He was, of course, stripped naked. Soon his right buttock was attacked and stabbed by a nurse with a syringe full of Thorozine. Such tender treatment was only awarded to docile, non-threatening volunteer patients. Recalcitrant sufferers got treated rudely.

0-595-24624-9